Dear Mystery Lover,

St. Martin's DEAD LETTER Paperback Mysteries are committed to bringing fresh new voices and series characters to the discriminating mystery readership. We view our relationship with our writers as a partnership: They write terrific books, we work with them to come up with the right copy and cover presentation, and we work together promoting each title to the mystery community. Every book and every writer is special to us, just as readers have a special relationship with the mystery writers they follow from book to book.

Graham Landrum's first novel *The Famous DAR Murder Mystery* is, quite simply, delightful. When a body is discovered in Borderville, Tennessee's Brown Spring Cemetery, the ladies of the Daughters of the American Revolution take up the case. If you love regional cozies or Miss Seeton or just love a charming homespun yarn, give the *DAR* a try. DEAD LETTER is also excited to be publishing Graham's *The Rotary Club Murder Mystery* and *The Sensational Music Club Mystery* in the months to come.

Keep your eye out for DEAD LETTER—and build yourself a library of paperback mysteries to die for.

Yours in crime,

Shawn Coyne
Editor
St. Martin's DEAD LETTER Paperback Mysteries

Upcoming Titles from St. Martin's Dead Letter Mysteries

THE *FAMOUS* D·A·R MURDER *MYSTERY*

GRAHAM LANDRUM

SMP

ST. MARTIN'S PAPERBACKS

THE FAMOUS DAR MURDER MYSTERY

Copyright © 1992 by Graham Landrum.

All rights reserved. No part of this book may be used or reproduced in any manner whatsoever without written permission except in the case of brief quotations embodied in critical articles or reviews. For information address St. Martin's Press, 175 Fifth Avenue, New York, N.Y. 10010.

Library of Congress Catalog Card Number: 91-33458

ISBN: 0-312-95568-5

Printed in the United States of America

St. Martin's Press hardcover edition published 1992
St. Martin's Paperbacks edition/July 1995

10 9 8 7 6 5 4 3 2

PREFACE

The author once had an aunt (she was a DAR) who lived alone. She dearly loved to read mysteries, but she did not like whodunits, in which murder was done in the course of the story. She much preferred that the mayhem be accomplished before the book began.

Now, that dear lady would have liked this story; for though there is murder in the middle of the book, the violence is played down.

The same lady loved genealogy as much as she loved detective fiction. Genealogy is the pursuit of hidden knowledge, and success at the end of the search is like the perfect outcome of a murder mystery.

Though his aunt has been dead for many years, the author has had her constantly in mind while writing the present yarn. It is his fervent hope that other ladies, especially DAR ladies, will enjoy this book.

The author has the highest regard for the National Society Daughters of the American Revolution. If he is occasionally amused by the Daughters, it is the amusement he has felt at the gentle behavior of his nearest and dearest: his grandmother, his aunt, his mother-in-law, and his wife—all loyal Daughters of the Revolution.

Long may the ladies of the DAR continue their good and patriotic work.

—GRAHAM LANDRUM
Bristol, Tennessee
10 July 1989

EXPLANATION

Isobel Parsons

By this time I suppose every man, woman, and child in the country knows about the famous DAR murder mystery. It has been in all the papers everywhere, and there can't be anybody who doesn't know already "who done it." And I hope that everybody knows that it was the Old Orchard Fort Chapter, NSDAR, in Borderville, Virginia, that solved the mystery and got 1,540 inches of publicity while doing it. That is just over 128 feet, and it is more publicity than any other chapter in the whole national society has ever received in any one year.

So why would anyone want to go through the whole thing again? And certainly I am nobody to set herself up as a *writer* of any kind, let alone mystery fiction—though of course this is not a made-up story, for it *really* happened. But Sarah Barnhouse made a motion at our September meeting that the whole affair ought to be written up.

Well, Elizabeth Wheeler had already pasted up all those

newspaper clippings in three big scrapbooks, and it did look as if that ought to be enough, but Sarah pointed out that about ninety percent of what was in the scrapbooks was just the *same* thing except that it came from different newspapers and the write-up in the *Atlanta Constitution* didn't really do justice to what our members had done.

Some of the members thought that Elizabeth had gone to so much work to paste up those scrapbooks that it would be a shame to go to any more bother. But Elizabeth herself said that even though the scrapbooks had all the main facts, it was very hard to get the connection from all those clippings. She had this great idea for each of the ladies to write up whatever it was she knew about, and then I was to put it together because I am the vice regent and don't have quite as much to do as the other officers. And so we all agreed that that was the thing to do—except Harriet Bushrow, who really solved the mystery. She said she had done enough and didn't want to write about it, but the members all insisted, and Harriet said she would.

I want to graciously thank all the daughters who have worked—I guess you would call it collaborated—on this project. All the ladies have written up their parts right away and just expressed themselves beautifully. So there hasn't been much for me to do except put the parts together and fill in a few gaps here and there.

Laverne Stalworthy typed it.

I do hope that people will like this story, and I'm happy to say that there is not any dirty language in it and no sex except the time that Harriet and Opal went to the nightclub to investigate the young men who do the striptease. But we *all* had to *laugh* about that because, after all, Harriet *uncovered* (ha! ha!) something there that was important in the case, and it was right in line with the national defense program that Opal had made the month before. It was real inspiration that led Harriet to that part of the investigation.

It's a great big book, as you can see. The Old Orchard Fort Chapter really has something to be proud of, and I hope it will give pleasure to many readers as well as wake us up and inform us about the dangers that threaten our nation today.

But first I want to point out the four ladies who carried the case through. To begin with, there is Helen Delaporte, our Regent. She is just a fine, fine regent, and nothing can stop her. Well, almost nothing—because she *did* stop when Mr. Delaporte just laid down the law and told her she absolutely could not go any further, and I know the reader will understand how that is.

Still, it was Helen right at the first who just pushed ahead in spite of all the discouragement she had. She is a wonderful example of how the DAR is an organization that *gets things done*.

Helen is a northern girl and came to Borderville about twenty years ago when Henry (Mr. Delaporte) joined Meagin, Meagin, and Johnston. Mr. Delaporte has done very well; and since old Mr. Meagin has been dead for many years, and Mr. Arthur Meagin, Jr., retired and went to Florida a number of years ago and Stubby Johnston is so crippled with arthuritus, Mr. Delaporte is the main part of the firm.

Helen doesn't seem like a Northerner at all. She is pretty and has lovely clothes, and she can do so many things that her time is always in demand. She has been regent of our chapter twice, and she was state registrar (we're a Virginia chapter, here in Borderville, being on the state line; and though Helen actually lives in Tennessee, she is the regent of a Virginia chapter). It's just amazing all the things she can do—a fine musician (she's organist and has the choir at the Episcopal church and plays at weddings *all* the time), and *smart* (she graduated from Vassar College)! And such a wonderful homemaker! Well—we're just fortunate to have her.

The other three ladies are Elizabeth Wheeler, Margaret Chalmers, and Harriet Bushrow. Together with Helen, they are the ones who found the body, found out who it was, did all that detecting, and finally it was Ms. Bushrow that solved the mystery. She is *eighty-six* years old! Well, that just shows what a DAR can do.

And now our story unfolds.

BROWN SPRING AND WHAT WE FOUND THERE

Helen Delaporte

We were looking for a dead man—one who had been buried over a century ago; and we found a dead man—one who had not been buried at all.

One of the activities of the DAR involves marking the graves of soldiers of the American Revolution. The national organization has rigid standards for this activity, and a local chapter may find that it takes a year or more to complete the required process. First we authenticate the soldier whose grave is to be marked. We find his record, which is usually not very difficult to do; but this calls for research and correspondence that can take several months. Then we must locate the grave as accurately as possible. Down here in southwestern Virginia and east Tennessee, many of the old soldiers were buried without gravestones or in graves that were marked with limestone or sandstone that has crumbled beyond recognition. "National" takes a reasonable attitude toward our problems. But we are all very anxious to be accurate, and

1

identifying unmarked or untended graves can be very difficult.

When the soldier has been researched and the grave located, a bronze marker is ordered and paid for by the chapter, and a ceremony is held at the grave when the marker is put in place.

The grave we were looking for was that of Adoniram Philipson. Philipson enlisted in 1778 at the age of seventeen and managed to be so severely wounded in his first battle that he was a cripple for life. It was a long life; and since Philipson died in 1851, and thus appeared in the 1850 census as a resident of Ambrose County, Virginia, we had assumed that we would find his grave without much search. He ought to have been with the rest of his family in the cemetery at Ambrose Courthouse.

But he was not. The chapter began work on poor old Adoniram in 1976 as a Bicentennial project. By the time Philipson died, there were few Revolutionary War veterans remaining; and Adoniram enjoyed considerable fame in our corner of the world. Thus there was an abundance of records. But we were absolutely balked when we tried to locate the grave.

We never quite gave the project up, but it was knocking around as unfinished business for almost ten years—until, in fact, I received a letter from George FitzSimmons Francis of Roanoke. Mr. Francis is very knowledgeable about southwest Virginia history; and in his researches he had found correspondence in which there was the sentence: "We laid Uncle Ad beside Cousin Emily Dunbar." The writer was Elizabeth Philipson Davis.

This information gave us a strong lead to follow because the Dunbars were a numerous family along the Holston where it flows into the state of Tennessee.

After some intense research, our Elizabeth Wheeler turned

up evidence that Emily Dunbar was a daughter of Adoniram Philipson's youngest sister. And when Elizabeth reported this to our November meeting last year, Margaret Chalmers, who grew up in the valley, announced that the Dunbars, although they had died out or moved away long before her time, were buried in great numbers in the Brown Spring Cemetery. And wonder of wonders, the Brown Spring Cemetery is just barely above the Tennessee line. Otherwise a Virginia chapter would be unable to mark the grave.

We learned all of that in the November meeting and were so encouraged that I thought we ought to complete this business right away.

With the Christmas music, however, and gifts, and cards—not to mention family—and with perfectly horrible weather in January, I felt that Adoniram's grave could go unmarked at least until we had a few sunny days.

The first such day came on February 22—Washington's *real* birthday, and a Tuesday. The sun was just rising clear over the knobs—it had not done so for three weeks—as Henry was getting off to the office. It seemed to me that all things were auspicious.

I called Margaret Chalmers, indispensable because she would have to pilot me to the cemetery. Yes, she could go—she would be glad to get out of the house.

Then because Elizabeth Wheeler was not only on the committee, but also because she enjoys cemeteries more than any other person I have ever known, I called her; and she could go.

I have to confess that I hesitated before I called Harriet Bushrow. If I had not called her, we might never have solved the mystery. But that is neither there nor there, because I called her although I had a qualm about taking her to such a place as the Brown Spring Cemetery. She is eighty-six and had a serious bout with flu in January. She is not as steady on her feet as she used to be. She is not actually large—that is to say not remarkably so—but because of the terrain we might encounter and the flu she had just had, I was afraid there might be difficulty.

Then I told myself that undoubtedly Harriet had been shut up in the house for several weeks and it would really be good for her to get out. There is, of course, a certain friction between Harriet and Elizabeth; and I suppose I had better explain why.

In order to join the DAR, one must be able to prove her legitimate descent from someone who fought on the American side in the Revolution or someone who furnished material aid to the colonists. After descent has been proved, she "goes in" on such-and-such as ancestor. The daughter then wears on her blue and white DAR ribbon a gold bar with the ancestor's name and rank engraved on it. If the daughter has other revolutionary ancestors, she may send proof to National and wear additional ancestor bars. Some daughters take great pride in the number of bars decorating their ribbons.

Elizabeth Wheeler has thirty-two bars!

That is, in fact, one gold bar for every male ancestor of military age in her entire lineage at the time of the Revolution. And she has three other ancestors she could claim in cases where both father and son aided the colonists.

I don't know that Elizabeth is unique in this matter, but it is a rare daughter that glitters as she does when she drapes her ribbons over her modest little chest. On the other hand, there is not a single commissioned officer in the whole collection. As Elizabeth herself will say, they were very ordinary people. But she will add that they all did their duty and—what is more important for her purposes—left a record of it.

Harriet, on the other hand! Well, Harriet has only three bars, and it rankles, because Harriet Gardner Bushrow is decidedly aristocratic with glamorous ancestors that far outshine Elizabeth's. One was Major General Archibald Hadley, and another was Lieutenant General Nathan Andrews. But Harriet can secure ancestral bars for neither of these. General Andrews, being somewhat older than Hadley, had a beautiful daughter. After the war Hadley was so captivated by Miss Andrews that he eloped with her, leaving behind a legal Mrs. Hadley and several small and very legitimate Hadleys. The Hadley-Andrews alliance prospered without benefit of law, and the descendants married into the best families. Since Harriet's mother was twice a Hadley (that is, there was a marriage of cousins a few generations ago), the two generals appear twice in her ancestry and thus eliminate four possible bars.

Physically too, Harriet and Elizabeth are as different as can be. Elizabeth is somewhat under five feet tall and weighs in the neighborhood of ninety in her galoshes. At seventy-five, she is a lively, bright-eyed retired domestic science teacher, who always wears a little dark suit and a white shirt waist with ruffled collar and cuffs.

Harriet, on the other hand, seems to have inherited the military bearing of her famous and illegitimate ancestors. Even now she can draw herself up and be the handsomest figure in the room.

Although Harriet's house is neither large nor old—and I might add that it is very plain—she has furnished it with moveables of museum quality—not at all the usual personal collection, for she had nothing made after 1830 or originating at a distance greater than one hundred miles of the Virginia-Tennessee border.

Harriet wears pronounced colors—a good strong rose, forest green, or russet—and hats with wide brims, always sloping at a raffish angle so that she looks like a duchess by Leley or even Van Dyck. And there is always her cut crystal necklace of which she is so fond.

Enough about Harriet. Now let me say something about Margaret Chalmers.

Of course, there's really not much to say about Margaret. Her husband sold life insurance and apparently bought his own policies, because he died about twenty years ago and left Margaret in comfortable condition. She has no children, but she makes up for that deficiency with nieces, nephews, old aunts and uncles, and endless cousins. I am very fond of Margaret. If possible, I like to have her share a room with me at State Conference.

By the time I had collected everybody in the Pontiac and got on the Valley Pike, it was two-thirty. Since we were going into Margaret's special part of the county, she had her local history well in hand and was eager to entertain us with it.

"Helen," she began in her soft voice, "did you know that Dr. Edmond Spooner camped at Brown Spring in seventeen fifty-eight?"

Seventeen fifty-eight marks the first authenticated exploration of our area.

I: "Did he?"

Elizabeth: "He did." This came with great authority, for that is the sort of thing that Elizabeth knows.

Margaret: "Grandfather Weathered's big log house burned, but the chimneys are still standing. You can see them over there on the left."

Elizabeth: "My ancestor, George Bennington, was a mason; he made half the chimneys in Chinahook County, Father used to say."

I: "How interesting!"

Thus my conversation alternated with the two, each of the ladies contributing scraps of information known only to themselves and leaving Harriet as completely out of it as if she had stayed at home. Harriet, you see, grew up in South Carolina and has no family ties to our local area.

Harriet's silence was icy. When I glimpsed her in the rearview mirror, that big hat was drooping over her face so that all I could see was the firm set of her jaw and her cut crystal beads flashing as she breathed.

We got behind a school bus just coming out from the Valley Pike Elementary School. As the bus stopped at every farm house, Margaret would recognize at least one child in each group that left the vehicle. This led to an individual detail of family history each time we came to a halt; and since Valley Pike is excessively crooked and also narrow, I had no chance to pass.

Elizabeth, on the other hand, found a way to enlarge the genealogical information related in every story contributed by Margaret. From time to time Harriet made an effort to start a different conversation.

Harriet: "Helen, do you like the Plymouth?"

I: "This is a Pontiac, Harriet."

Harriet: "Oh!"

After another five minutes of Margaret's local history enlarged by Elizabeth's footnotes, Harriet would try again.

Harriet: "Helen, do you find your heating bills high this year?"

We followed Valley Pike to Hipple's Store, then turned on Farm Road 17 until we reached the Hersey place, a grand old log house with clapboard siding and additions in all directions. The oaks are even older than the house and spread above it with great gnarled branches. At Margaret's direction I turned off onto a dirt road, which served well until we passed the Billy Pennybacker place, where the ruts became downright unpleasant and I began to worry about my shock absorbers. I drove on, dead slowly, for about ten minutes— back into the knobs. Margaret pointed out where the Brown

Spring Church had stood before it was torn down, and we could see Brown Branch meandering off through the fields. At last we came to a rusty fence and a huge arch made of pipe with a somewhat battered sign hanging from its apex to tell us that we had arrived at the Brown Spring Cemetery. It was rather a pretty cemetery, cut out of the woods and lying between two knobs to the right and to the left. It was somewhat larger than I had expected it would be. Immediately in front of us there was a grassy slope crowned with monuments and stones—leaning this way and that, but always expectantly facing east. Perhaps thirty yards beyond the gate there was a slight rise, and apparently the cemetery sloped around on the other side and continued a short distance up the hollow.

The cemetery association had done an efficient job on the weeds and brambles, and I was relieved to see that I need not have feared that my ladies could not negotiate the terrain.

I am always impressed by the quiet of a country cemetery, and apparently so were my passengers; for as the Pontiac's engine died, our conversation died also.

We disembarked and entered almost timidly—perhaps with the feeling that we were intruding. Quietly we made our way through the gate, the only sound beside our footsteps resulting from Harriet's opening her purse to get a cough drop.

Suddenly Elizabeth broke our reverie with a polite shriek—"Hunsuckers!"

It sounded as though we were being warned of something—possibly a bird that would swoop down and attack us.

"And there's another one!"

Elizabeth is in her personal element in a cemetery, and we could tell that she was prepared to be delighted by this one.

"I have Hunsuckers!"

"Elizabeth Wheeler," Harriet said with annoyance, "What on earth are you talking about?"

"Great-Uncle John Payne married a Hunsucker," Elizabeth explained. "And just look at them!"

"Yes, there were a lot of them," said Margaret.

"Well," Harriet said, slightly out of humor, "by all means let Elizabeth collect her Hunsuckers while the rest of us locate Adoniram Philipson."

We did in fact find Adoniram Philipson. He was among the trees just outside the fence, which was perhaps put up at some time after Adoniram went to his long home. The stone was broken, lying face down and almost buried. It had apparently been in that condition for many years. But since it was only a fragment and the whole stone had not been very large anyhow, I had no trouble prying it up and turning it over. We felt ourselves very fortunate to be able to read:

ADON. PHI
BORN 1760—DI

I took shelf paper and a cobbler's heel from a shopping bag I always carry when I go to a cemetery. A rubbing makes the report a little more interesting to the chapter. I taped the paper to the stone and began rubbing briskly as Harriet and Margaret watched.

Suddenly we heard a stage whisper from Elizabeth and saw her running toward us at a strange little tiptoe pace.

"There is a man up there," she said in an excited whisper. "I think he needs help."

"Well, Elizabeth," Harriet boomed, "did you offer to help him?"

"I did clear my throat," Elizabeth said, "but he didn't move. He's lying partly behind a tombstone. I didn't get too close."

Harriet, always the descendant of generals, led off firmly as I put my rubbing equipment into my market bag. Elizabeth and Margaret followed Harriet, and I brought up the rear—somewhat like the barnyard friends of Chicken Little.

At the peak of the slight rise, Elizabeth pointed to a tombstone with MOTHER carved across it in huge letters. Visible from behind one side of it, a pair of legs in blue jeans sprawled at an unnatural angle. A Jack Daniel's bottle lay about a yard away.

When I arrived on the scene, so to speak, Harriet was breathing heavily from her exertion, but she had drawn herself up to her full height, while the other two ladies somehow seemed smaller than themselves. They were a little to the rear of Harriet and gave the impression of frightened children peeking around their mother's skirts.

"I suppose he's drunk," Margaret said.

"Why, he is plainly dead!" Harriet announced as though only a fool would suppose otherwise.

"But perhaps he isn't. Do you suppose we should see if there is a pulse?" Margaret murmured so gently and timidly that I didn't hesitate to go through the motions I vaguely remembered from a long-forgotten course in first aid, saying "hello" loudly and feeling for a pulse.

Of course Harriet was right. The poor man had been attacked savagely about the neck, the lower face, and the left temple with something heavy enough to be frightfully lethal. The eyes were open, and at this point of my examination I discovered something quite surprising. Those eyes did not match. One was brown, very dark, staring at me in the manner of a dead fish. The pupil of the other eye was strange—not clear—as though there were a film across it.

There on my knees, holding that clammy hand, I was aware of two things: first that there was absolutely no pulse; and second that his hand was quite limp, which I realized later meant that rigor mortis had passed.

Even at that time I assumed that the man had been dead for a good while.

I never supposed I would have such an experience, and I certainly would never have been able to guess what my reaction would be. What happened was that the names of my favorite detective fiction authors passed through my mind: Agatha Christie, Marjorie Allingham, Dorothy Sayers. What would Inspector Appleby do in this case? How strange my reaction seems! After all, I am essentially a housewife and a church organist.

Although I wouldn't say that my memory is photographic, nevertheless it is visual. I can look closely at anything, and if I concentrate while I am looking at it, I can recall visually whatever I have observed in that way. I do this when I memorize music. And I was fixing in my visual memory what I was seeing at that time. I noted the peculiarities of the head, the eyes, the ears, the contusions, the clothing—which I immediately saw could not have been intended for this man—and the hands.

Hands tell so much about a person. Although dressed in filthy ragged clothing much too large for him, this man had clean hands. His nails were immaculate, rounded sensibly—and lacquered with clear nail polish. I was so surprised by this detail that I turned the hands over and examined the palms and the tips of the fingers—strong fingers; and there was a callus at each fingertip.

"We must call the sheriff," I said. Though only slightly north of the Tennessee line, we were of course in Virginia, (an obvious necessity if the grave is to be marked by a Virginia chapter); and so it was the sheriff on the Virginia side that must be notified.

"We can phone from Billy Pennybacker's place," Margaret volunteered, her voice not loud but alive with shock and excitement. Surely the Old Orchard Fort Chapter had never been involved in anything like this. We made our way back to the Pontiac and crawled down that rutted lane, about three quarters of a mile.

Rachel Pennybacker is a handsome woman of about sixty-five. Long a friend of Margaret, she opened her house to the four of us with immediate hospitality and great interest in our sensational discovery. We trooped through to her old-fashioned kitchen, where the phone was, and took possession.

The deputy who answered my call told us to stay where we were until the sheriff could get there.

Mrs. Pennybacker put a pot of coffee on the stove, and we discussed first the unknown dead man in the cemetery, then Adoniram Philipson, African violets, Sears appliances, and finally the Pennybacker grandchildren. At that point Harriet announced that she would visit the lavatory. Mrs. Pennybacker offered to take her upstairs to show her where the bathroom was, but Harriet firmly insisted that she could find it herself. Margaret gave me a knowing look, because we all know that if Harriet says she wants to use the bathroom, it usually means that she is going to explore the house.

Ten minutes later Harriet returned to us and said to our hostess, "I couldn't help noticing your cannonball bed. I suppose it was in your family?"

It was, and the conversation readily turned into a lecture on candle stands, clothespresses, mule-eared chairs, and band-boxes.

Finally, when Sheriff Gilroy arrived with Deputy Lassiter, Margaret, Elizabeth, and I left Harriet at the Pennybacker place because of her recent recovery from flu and returned to the cemetery.

The sheriff's car preceded mine; and when we got to the cemetery fence, the sheriff's radio was squawking away to let us know that a TV crew was on its way. This would be a treat for Channel Five. Our station has a hard time filling up its local news program and is always delighted with any gruesome event to fling at the public.

A good many things began to happen, and it was a long, drawn-out process. I was glad that Henry had an evening meeting of the library board and would not be home for dinner.

When I finally got to the house, I felt as if I had been gone a week. I took a hot bath, threw on a robe, made myself a tuna sandwich, and tried to work on the music for Holy Week, but it was hard to put the events of the day out of my mind.

At a quarter to ten I turned on the TV to Channel Five for the local news. I sat there through Ed Asher's Chevrolet ad, the efforts of the Boys Club to raise money for weight-lifting equipment, the little old lady on the Virginia side who had won $20,000 in the lottery, and then—the only grisly event of the day—our discovery at Brown Spring Cemetery.

They gave us almost eight minutes with shots of the cemetery, shots of the body covered with a black cloth, and a glimpse of me in the background. There was a good shot of Margaret, quite a lot of Sheriff Butch Gilroy blustering around, and finally a very good interview with Elizabeth.

I wish National could have seen that interview, because Elizabeth handled it beautifully. She explained fully and clearly what the DAR is and does. She included our support of schools, particularly the ones we own, like our Kate Duncan Smith DAR School in Alabama. And she spoke of the scholarships we give in American history, government, nursing, and occupational therapy. And of course she explained about locating and marking the graves of Revolutionary soldiers and patriots. There was a shot of the fragment of Philipson's headstone, and Elizabeth was in her glory explaining who he was in the most minute detail; and yet she did it all charmingly.

Since Elizabeth has been one of our best publicity chairmen for many years in the past, she knew exactly what to do, giving the name of our chapter—Old Orchard Fort—several times and linking the afternoon's events to the legitimate activities of the NSDAR.

I was still grinning like the cat who had been in the cream when Henry came home a few minutes later.

He had had a long and troublesome meeting at the library and was tired, but he revived considerably when I began to tell him what had happened in my life since he had last seen me.

I began at the very beginning and went through every detail. The telecast and my visual memory brought it back to me with absolute clarity.

"Henry," I said when I had finished my story, "that poor man had the most beautiful hands!"

"Beautiful hands!" Henry exclaimed. "Are you talking about the dead? The dead man!"

"Yes, he must have been an extraordinary person."

"De mortuis nil nisi bonum," Henry said. "You found him charming, I dare say." He treats me this way sometimes.

"Charming," I echoed. There is no point in resisting Henry's sarcasm. "Perhaps he was not as conversational as he might have been," I added.

It was the discordance of the thing—the hands so carefully groomed. Nothing would lead one to expect such hands. Not the clothing, which was three or four sizes too big—not the discarded Jack Daniel's bottle. Nor did the manner of death go with the hands. I told Henry what I was thinking.

"Let the sheriff worry about that," he said.

I followed Henry to bed. In the morning the *Banner-Democrat* had a story on the front page as follows:

CITY WOMEN FIND CORPSE IN CEMETERY

Members of a local women's organization were surprised to find the body of an unknown man apparently killed in a drunken brawl. "I never was so surprised in my life," said Ms. Elizabeth Wheeler, who discovered the body. "There he was lying behind a tombstone."

Sheriff Calvin ("Butch") Gilroy reported that no identification was found on the body and assumes that the deceased was a transient. "Two or three of them probably got drunk and started a fight," Gilroy speculated. "We get lots of this."

The attack upon the deceased was directed at the face and throat apparently with a blunt object. County Coroner Donald R. Woolwine reported that the death was caused by rupture of the thorax.

I said to Henry, who was reading the editorial page, "Butch Gilroy is going to attribute everything to a fight between drunks and forget about it."

"Oh yes, that business out at Brown Spring," Henry said. "It wouldn't surprise me at all."

"Well," I said, thinking it over. "I was on the ground; I know as much about it as Butch Gilroy; and I say he is wrong. And I don't like his cavalier attitude. He obviously expects to dismiss the whole thing as if it didn't matter." Gilroy belongs to a fraternal order or two. When the B.O.P. brings the circus here, he dresses up like a clown, gets on the tube, and begs us all to buy tickets so that underprivileged children can see the show. He boosts the high-school teams—which is all very well; but he does as little work in the sheriff's office as possible unless he can appear on television. When election time comes around, he is to be seen with a toothy grin all over town. I do not like him.

Henry had now turned to the market reports. I could tell by the way he was holding the paper that he had got down to Pennsylvania Power and Light. Henry is a darling man, but he tends to overlook me at times, and I sometimes don't appreciate that.

"Henry!"

"Yes?"

"Well, it was a murder, you know; and it has to be taken as seriously as it would be taken if the victim had been the president of the Planters Trust Bank"

"Oh, yes," he said, lowering his paper. "In theory crimes should never go unpunished. But you know, my dear, there are crimes that cannot be explained and therefore cannot be punished. And a casual crime such as this one appears to be is the most hopeless situation that law enforcement can face: an unknown—in an out-of-the-way place that has no logical connection with the murdered individual or with the crime—is killed in a fight with another unknown, who has never been on the scene before and will never be on the scene again. No witnesses. No suspects. No motive. What can you expect of a sheriff like Gilroy—a good old boy who is dumb enough to like being sheriff and smart enough to hang on to the job. He hasn't got enough money in his budget to hire a staff capable of handling the routine cases that come his way. Even if he put half his force on a hopeless case like this, he would have to draw men from other duty where they are actually serving the county and send them on this goose chase. There is no possible satisfactory conclusion for a case like this, and he probably feels that there are better ways to spend his time and the taxpayers' money."

"You, Henry Delaporte," I said, "have told me times without number about the responsibility of the law to extend

equal protection to every citizen, no matter who he is or how
unable he is to pay a lawyer. You even addressed the chapter
during Constitution Week on this very topic. How can you
sit there and condone a system that protects the rights of a
man who's known in the community and ignores a stranger?"

"I know, but the casual murder of a bum is not at all likely
to be solved."

I thought that one over a second while Henry returned to
his paper.

"He was not a bum," I said.

"He had beautiful hands," Henry mumbled, his head still
in the paper.

"And he was murdered casually by hoodlums—in the
Brown Spring Cemetery?" I continued. Look—he must have
been murdered somewhere else. There is no other possibil-
ity." I could not get the inconsistencies out of my mind.
Those misfit clothes . . . They couldn't have been his.

Inhaling the fumes from my coffee, I reexamined that
picture I had summoned to my mind. I could see the face that
had been so severely battered—such gashes on that face—and
yet it now occurred to me that there was no blood on the
shirt. It came to me, as things do, like a picture. And then I
noticed something that I had not noticed before.

"Henry, there's something else."

"All right, what?" Henry reached across the table and took
the section of the paper that had been lying in front of me.

"He had quite a tan."

"Don't most bums have a tan?"

"He was clean-shaven and had a tan—like a tan a man
might get on a golf course."

"Oh, come on! Your imagination is out of control, my
dear."

"The tan went right on up to his bald head, which wasn't
tanned at all."

"The man wore a hat."

"Yes, I suppose so." And yet there was a distinct line where the hair should have begun, but perhaps Henry was right. Perhaps I was playing my game too hard. I concentrated on my coffee.

A cup of good coffee usually puts dreamy things into my head. So I tried to think of something more pleasant. What the poor murdered man might perhaps have looked like before he was so savagely battered. I visualized him in evening clothes. As I saw him, he was rather handsome. I made him out to be about fifty. There he was—but with that bald head! Then something in my brain clicked. The sensitive hands, the white tie and tails, and perhaps a toupee—bowing after a performance of some kind. Then I thought about the calluses on his fingers. There was a clue there. Certain musicians, such as guitarists, have such calluses. Whatever might be the truth, I was convincing myself more and more of my original statement. "He was not a bum," I insisted.

Henry laughed. "All right, my dear, your man was a very important fellow, but you'll have a hard time convincing the sheriff of that."

That was Wednesday. Wednesday means choir practice, and I had laundry to do and a thousand other things to take care of. There was no time to consider the DAR mystery any further. Besides, it was still very much an imaginary adventure to me, and I didn't expect to think seriously about it again.

HOW THE OLD ORCHARD FORT CHAPTER GOT SO MUCH PUBLICITY

Elizabeth Wheeler

Isobel Parsons insists that I must write up everything that I did in connection with the murder business that our chapter worked out. My part of it was really very small. Being the first in the group to actually see the body might count for something. But I would never have the courage of Helen Delaporte, the Regent of the Old Orchard Fort Chapter, who examined the body really in a most professional way and did so many things that I would never have dared to do. And then, of course Mrs. Bushrow was so clever and brave. I just have to think there was some purpose that brought those two ladies together that day in the Brown Spring Cemetery, because neither I nor Margaret would have known what to do.

On the other hand, having two jobs in the chapter—I am public relations chairman and also on the committee that helps the ladies with their genealogy—it turned out that there were two things I could do to help.

From a very small child, I have always been interested in

family history. I love old records and feel that there is nothing more exciting than uncovering forgotten facts by means of faded old documents, letters found in neglected trunks, old Bibles, and a thousand and one memories that have been handed down from our ancestors. But that part of my work comes later in the story. The thing for me to explain now is how the Old Orchard Fort Chapter got 1,540 inches of publicity in one year.

Actually I was not supposed to be public relations chairman this year. Frances St. John was chairman; but when her son moved to Florida, she went with him and resigned the chairmanship. So since I had been public relations chairman about five years ago, I agreed to step in, little suspecting what it would lead to.

National is very strict about giving credit for publicity. The newspaper—oh, how they can get things wrong! They must—absolutely must—print the name of the chapter accurately. It is not enough to say, "The DAR did so and so, or "a local chapter of the DAR did this." I remember once that I inserted a story in the paper and they changed "Old Orchard Fort Chapter, NSDAR" to "an old chapter of the DAR." So we got no credit although the story ran nine inches.

Well, here's how I got 1,540 inches of publicity and got it all counted for the Old Orchard Fort Chapter.

I have a recipe for pound cake that I got from a cousin in Russell County. I think it's about the best pound cake at all, and I've noticed whenever I've served it where there were men, my pound cake disappeared faster than anything else on the table. It is not at all hard to make; and since I don't have to ice it, it's easy to carry in the car. So that's the cake I generally make when there has been a death somewhere or they want a cake at the church or anything in that line.

Not to go into too many details, I got just very busy; and

the cake turned out to be lovely—as it always does. Besides, I love the smell of it while it's baking.

Then I got all dolled up and took my cake down to the newspaper office.

I asked the young lady at the big desk—the one just after you go through the main door—I asked her who the reporter was that had written up the story about our little escapade. It turned out that it was a nice young man—new on the paper—named Albert Manley.

Of course I used to be very chummy with Kate Loveless when she was on the paper, and I trained her to handle DAR publicity and notices and that kind of thing, though she made some awful mistakes sometimes. But she died about three years ago. Anyhow, this young man was quite a different item from Kate.

Well, the young lady at the front desk I was telling about directed me toward the back of the building, where there was a big room with nice windows all along the south side and a good many desks all neatly lined up. And one of them belonged to this good-looking young man named Albert Manley.

I guess I was a little hesitant, because it was just a little bit "forward" of me to do what I was going to do.

I said, "Good morning!" and, "I'm Elizabeth Wheeler." And he stood up right away and was very polite.

He said, "I'm Albert Manley," and, "Won't you sit down?"

So I did, holding my big cake box on my lap.

"Would you like to rest that package on my desk?" he said.

So I did, and I took the top off the box.

"See what this is?" I said. "Would you like to have a piece?

"Oh, don't cut your cake," he said, and I could tell right away that his mother had raised him right.

"But that's what I made it for," I said, and I commenced

cutting it with the cake break that I had slipped into the side of the box.

About that time everyone else in the room seemed to know what was going on. All the typewriters or word processors or whatever those things are called stopped rattling and all those faces were looking at me and Mr. Manley, and especially at my cake.

"I imagine there is enough for everybody," I said. So they all crowded around. It was just the way I knew it would be. That pound cake never fails.

"I want you all to know that this pound cake is a bribe," I told them. "I have a recipe for Belgrade bread that I bet you would all like. And I'll make it for you if you'll do something nice for me."

Of course Mr. Manley and all of them wanted to know what that was—which gave me an opening to explain how I wanted them to write up anything that was said about our chapter. I made them understand that the name of the chapter is most important and that the story must show that the chapter is engaged in a DAR-related activity.

Then I explained about marking the grave of Adoniram Philipson, which is a bona fide activity of our chapter, and we ought to get credit for any story that mentions it and mentions it in the right way. And I gave Mr. Manley my DAR year-book so that he can always get the names right, and asked him please, please to always call me when he was going to write something about our chapter so I could say the publicity came from us, which of course it did.

I could tell immediately that the Old Orchard Fort Chapter, DAR, would feature in every news story in the *Bordertown Banner-Democrat* if there was any connection at all with that matter out at Brown Spring.

Now just in case some other chapter wants to bribe the newspaper, here is the recipe:

BUTTERMILK POUND CAKE

3 cups flour	6 eggs separated
3 cups sugar	½ teaspoon salt
1 cup shortening	¼ teaspoon soda
1 cup buttermilk	2 teaspoons lemon or
	orange flavoring

Blend sugar and shortening. Add egg yolks, one at a time, and blend after each addition. Add flavoring. Sift dry ingredients together and add to first mixture alternately with buttermilk. Begin and end with dry ingredients. Beat egg whites until stiff and carefully fold into mixture. Pour batter into 10-inch tube pan, greased and floured. Bake at 350 about 1 hour and 10 minutes.

And of course you can bake it in a Bundt pan, and the cake will be very pretty on a stand even though it is not iced.

HOW I CAME TO BE AT
CROSS-PURPOSES
WITH OUR SHERIFF

Helen Delaporte

The following day, which was Thursday, there was a short follow-up story in the *Banner-Democrat* that simply said that no identification of our "DAR" corpse had been made and that no missing persons had been reported who corresponded to our man, although an inquiry had been received from Shelby County. What surprised me was seeing the full name of our chapter, my name as regent, and an explanation of our mission, i.e., locating a Revolutionary War grave in order to mark it. As a recap of the story that had appeared before, it seemed an unusually long story. I did not know then to what depths Elizabeth had stooped to secure our publicity.

Later I called Sheriff Gilroy and told him all the things I had noticed about the corpus delicti. He was polite to me because he was coming up for election and had not yet figured out how he could fob me off. I knew immediately that although he was listening with elaborate patience and politeness, he was not really hearing a word. Henry does the same thing sometimes, and there is nothing that makes me so mad.

"This man was not just a derelict," I said.

Gilroy said, "Now, Ms. Delaporte"—I can't stand to be called *Ms.*—"we have a lot of cases like this. Bums break into a fishing cabin—a hunting cabin—they steal liquor. . ."

"What fishing cabin? What hunting cabin?" I demanded. I am not so stupid as to suppose that every stolen bottle of Jack Daniel's is reported to the sheriff, but in this case the fishing cabins and hunting cabins occupied a position only in Gilroy's imagination and were constructed on the spur of the moment expressly to get me out of his hair. It was a totally unsatisfactory conversation. I was so provoked that I went around most of the day with my lower lip stuck out. When Henry came home, he said, "What's the matter? What's wrong?"

"Oh, nothing," I answered quite firmly, as I always do when I am in a sulk, and Henry knew enough not to ask further.

Nothing much happened for the rest of the week.

Sunday is my big day. I try to get to the church early to run over the prelude and postlude before anyone shows up. Then, by good fortune, the 8:00 o'clock communion is a read service; and while it is going on, I get to have another cup of coffee and do a few things in the choir room, such as put the chairs back where they are supposed to be, put out the anthems, check the choir robes, etc. Meanwhile I wonder how many choristers will show up and hope that my old Hillgreen and Lane won't develop a cipher.

But I always get through the service, and I really feel that I have accomplished something when I get to the last few bars of the postlude. I reach over and press the switch, and the organ goes dead. I look up, and the church is almost empty except for me and the altar guild.

But that Sunday—it was the twenty-seventh—I looked up

and there was Elizabeth Wheeler in her little black hat with the pheasant feathers shooting across it.

"Dear, the music was so pretty!"

Whether I play Bach, Mendelssohn, or Messiaen, they always say it is "pretty."

I make it a practice to say (as I said to Elizabeth) thank you, and I try to say it prettily.

Elizabeth was fishing about in a huge black purse, out of which she pulled what seemed to be a brochure that had fallen for an instant into a rain-filled gutter.

"Here's your map, dear."

"My map?"

"Yes, it must have fallen out of the car when we got out at the cemetery. I picked it up and slipped it into my purse and forgot to give it to you."

I recognized the folded paper as the map of Ambrose County. I took it because Elizabeth was handing it to me; but as I did so, I said, "That isn't mine. I have one somewhere, but this isn't mine."

"But it was right beside your car, and it must have fallen out."

I opened the map and spread it out. It was still just a bit damp, though it was probably not so wet as to affect anything in Elizabeth's purse. "Someone must have lost it in the snow," I said. "When did that snow fall, anyhow?"

"Saturday—I think—yes, a week ago yesterday."

And then I remembered. Choir directors always remember when it snows on weekends.

Now that I had opened the map, I saw a heavy pencil line marking the route from Borderville to the Brown Spring Cemetery.

Could this be Margaret's? But no—I couldn't imagine her needing a map of an area that she knew so well. "Surely it wouldn't be Harriet's. I'll take it and ask her about it," I said as I put it with my music.

When I got home, I called Margaret. As I had assumed, Margaret knew nothing about a map, and neither did Harriet.

But there it was—not actually grungy as though it had been exposed to the elements for weeks—but certainly dropped just outside the cemetery before the snow on the previous Saturday.

Here was an additional mystery, however minor. Could it be a clue? And if so, what did it mean?

The map, the Jack Daniel's bottle, and the body—the only three things that could tell us anything about the crime in that snowy cemetery on the previous Saturday.

This additional bit of evidence was a clue; but what did it mean?

I felt certain that the Jack Daniel's bottle had been placed deliberately to confuse any investigation. But the map was different: It surely must have been left accidently and therefore must be a genuine clue.

As I stood there looking at it, I realized that the map had been marked to show how to get *to* Brown Spring, but tracing the penciled line in the other direction led only to the city limit, where the line stopped—or, more properly, started.

What the the map proved was that someone who was unfamiliar with the district had gone to Brown Spring before that Saturday—the nineteenth, that would be—but not a very long time before the nineteenth.

I kept thinking about that map for the rest of the day. It seemed to me that the map said that the murder had been committed somewhere else and that someone familiar with the area had directed a second party—someone who was not familiar with the area—to Brown Spring in order to deposit the body in the cemetery. With the body thus remote, it would not have been discovered in the ordinary course of events for a month or more. And by that time decomposition and the superficial evidence of the bottle and the clothes would have convinced almost anybody that the man had been a mere bum who met misadventure at the hands of another bum. As things stood, therefore, it seemed obvious that someone had been at pains to remove the body from the place where the murder had occurred and put it in the Brown Spring Cemetery.

My citizenship hackles began to rise. Under our government every individual's life is of the greatest value. And if that life is taken away, is it not the duty of every citizen to see that justice is done? We talk a lot about rights and that sort of thing, but few people do anything about them. And so, like an idealistic teenager—more exactly an opinionated matron—I made up my mind to prod Butch Gilroy into making a decent inquiry.

It was still very much on my mind the next day.

Monday is a day when I usually try to get a little housecleaning done. But since I don't particularly like cleaning the house, I frequently start all sorts of projects on Monday because I think I have a whole week ahead with lots of time to do the unpleasant.

Henry was not coming home for dinner because he had a lot to do at the office and was going to grab a hamburger before going to the vestry meeting at 7:30. Consequently I did not have to think of more than a cup of soup and a sandwich for myself. All of this contributed to my illusion that I had time to spend as I wished.

All morning as I dusted the furniture, used the vacuum, and ran the mop over the floors I carried on a conversation with myself: Should I or should I not?

Then about one-thirty I thought I just might go out to Brown Spring and look around again. Of course that was just a way to put off the decision whether I would talk to Gilroy again or not.

So I went.

The area where we found the body had been trampled

pretty thoroughly—first by ourselves, then by Gilroy's men, and finally by the television crew. The Jack Daniel's bottle was there where someone had kicked it aside—additional proof that Gilroy had no intention of investigating the case.

As it turned out, we did not need the bottle as evidence, but I picked it up anyhow, being very careful not to add fingerprints.

I took my time wandering around the cemetery. There were at least two hundred graves there, representing for the most part perhaps twenty families, some of whom no doubt had either died out or vanished without trace during the hundred and fifty years that the cemetery has been used. Outside of the descendants of these twenty or so families, hardly anyone would be expected to know about the Brown Spring Cemetery. I wondered how many people that would be.

I thought back over the scores of detective stories I have read in the last thirty years. Where was it the detectives always began? At the scene of the crime. Well, Brown Spring wasn't that. So I couldn't examine the scene of the crime.

What else did detectives do? The time when the crime was committed always seems to be of great importance.

I drove down to Rachel Pennybacker's place. She seemed to be an intelligent, factual sort of person. I like her. In fact I hope we are going to be able to get her to join our chapter.

With her house situated where it is, she would have to know about any traffic to or from the Brown Spring Cemetery. How much was there in the winter months, I asked.

"Just about none," she said. "The cemetery association comes out one Saturday in the summer and clears the weeds and brush off. Of course there are some Confederate graves there and the UDC marks them on Memorial Day. There hasn't been a burial there in ten years. I would say a car doesn't pass up that way more than once a month for any reason."

"Did anybody go by week before last"? I asked.

"I don't know. Friday and Saturday we weren't here," she said. "Bill and I went up to Tazewell to see our grandson play basketball—left here about three-thirty—Chris is six foot four! While we were at the game, the snow came on, and it snowed all that night and most of Saturday. It was eight inches up there, and we couldn't get out until Sunday morning. We got in here about three o'clock. And there wasn't nearly that much snow here, though sometimes our lane gets pretty bad. And before that, I don't remember any car passing our gate. I would have heard it if I had been in the house, especially at night."

Well, I thought, that was probably as close as I could get to establishing the time when the body was deposited in the cemetery.

As soon as I got home, I called Margeret Chalmers. She is the only person I know who keeps a diary.

Yes, indeed, Margaret had it written down. "Saturday Feb. 19: Began snowing lightly at 8:15 A.M." That was the entry. "I remember that it snowed off and on all day," she said. Margaret added that though she had not written it down, she had noticed that the sky was clear by the time her favorite program came on. "That's at six o'clock," she explained.

I thought I was coming along pretty well as a detective. I surmised that the body had been deposited in the Brown Spring Cemetery sometime after the Pennybackers left home at 3:30 on Friday afternoon and before the snow was deep enough that car tracks could be seen when the Pennybackers returned on Sunday, because of course they would have noticed. Considering the nature of the business, I thought it safe to say that the body was moved at any time from sundown Friday the eighteenth to sunup Saturday the nineteenth.

When Henry came home from the vestry meeting, I didn't

tell him what I had been up to. I was going to wait until I had everything worked out. Then I would spring it on him all at once.

So he had no chance then to tell me to mind my own business. Henry is a dear! He worries about me. But when he finally got home, it was too late to stop me. I had made up my mind. I had already drawn up the following chart:

Feb. 18, Friday: Pennybackers absent from home.
19, Saturday: Snow beginning in the morning—the body deposited early enough so that no tracks appeared when Pennybackers returned.
20, Sunday: Sunshine, snow melting.
21, Monday: All snow melted. (No footprints around the body.)
22, Tuesday: P.M. Body discovered—clothing damp—map found at that time was damp.

And that was my proof that the body was placed in the cemetery on Friday night. And allowing a reasonable time for the perpetrators to figure out their plans and put them into action, I concluded that the murder could have taken place as early as Thursday but was unlikely to have taken place earlier. That was as far as I could go in fixing the time of the murder.

I went on to the next and biggest problem—namely, who was the corpse? What was there about the body that could lead to identification?

I could start with the deep suntan.

Borderville is in the South, all right, but it could hardly be proved by our winter weather. November is a beautiful month. The hills and mountains are still ablaze with color and the sun is bright as a new penny. We have a real nip in our air like the fresh apple cider that is for sale at every roadside stand. We have our first snow about Thanksgiving, and from then on the weather saddens increasingly. Those of us who can't go to Florida grit our teeth and make up our minds to live through until the sun returns—really returns—and our Appalachian spring steals upon us. Then our Florida visitors return home brown and healthy and look down on us who turned white—etiolated, if you please—while the sun hid behind the leaden clouds of January and February.

Since *my* corpse had a glorious tan, my first reaction was to say Florida, but Arizona, California, or any part of the Gulf coast would have answered just as well. And of course there were the West Indies and a hundred other places.

If Florida or the Gulf coast was the right place, then my man probably drove up in his car. And if so, I supposed that his car would be found eventually and the ownership traced. I could perhaps check that out with the police.

If Arizona or the West Coast were involved, my man would have flown in, and his car would not be a means of tracing him.

Nearly everything that comes into our airport goes through Charlotte, North Carolina; and before that, anything from the west comes through Atlanta, and I would think our man would have arrived here on USAir. So that was something that I could try.

As soon as Henry went off to work the next morning, I called the courthouse and asked for the office that would know about abandoned vehicles. After three tries, I got the officer in charge of such matters.

"Was an abandoned vehicle found in this county at any time between February seventeenth and February twenty-first?" I asked.

"Please describe the vehicle," the voice replied.

"Just any vehicle," I said.

"Don't you even know what your own vehicle was like?"

"It is not my vehicle."

"Then why in hell are you wasting my time?"

I have always been able to grasp at some obscure bit of information when it was really necessary. It doesn't mean that I am intelligent or knowledgeable, but it is a knack that has enabled me to appear much smarter than I really am.

"I am making this request under the Freedom of Information Act," I announced with great firmness. Of course I have no notion that the act requires an officer in East Tennessee to give out information about his office routine; but then the man on the other end of the line did not know anything about it either.

In fact he said, "I beg your pardon."

"Indeed you should," I shot back. "Now just give me a list of all abandoned vehicles found in this county between February seventeenth and February twenty-first."

"Well," came a subdued answer, "the fact is they ain't been none. Say, lady, what is your name anyhow?"

At that I softly replaced the phone in its cradle.

Having learned so much from my brush with the Virginia sheriff's department, I made a call to the Tennessee sheriff's department, where I handled the matter with much more aplomb. There had been no abandoned cars in Tennessee either.

As for inquiries at the airport, it struck me that I might be more successful if I made them in person.

Our airport serves Borderville, Parsons City, and Cooksport because there is only one tract in the area that is basically flat enough to accommodate a modern landing field. Even at that, in order to lay out our runways, several hills had to be removed. But it is a beautiful airport. From the observation deck on a clear day you can see range after range of mountains, shade after shade of blue, stretched out like the backs of dragons on a Ming vase. The terminal is big and full of natural light. Our airport represents our region at its best, and we are all proud of it.

I pulled up at the post that spits out a ticket admitting vehicles to the parking lot. The barricade rose, and I found a place near the steps leading down to the terminal building. The doors flew open before me, and I marched in, pretending far more assurance that I actually had.

I learned long ago not to apologize or hesitate when I am asking for a privilege or breaking a regulation. I simply demand—in a ladylike manner, of course—as though I am accustomed to deference, and smile benignly. Sometimes it works, and sometimes it doesn't. Nevertheless I still get butterflies in my stomach when I try such a thing.

Seeing no customers at the Delta desk, I breezed purposefully thither and said in a tone that could be heard throughout the foyer: "I should like to know who was at this desk on the afternoon of February eighteenth."

The young woman behind the counter was unnaturally blond, very chic, and thickly painted. She looked the picture of self-possession. But so did I, and I took encouragement from the fact that her act was a sham just as mine was.

"I was," she said.

"Then perhaps you can help me," I said without lowering my voice. "I am asking about a passenger coming through Charlotte—male, about fifty-five or sixty, five foot ten, well dressed"—of course I was guessing—"brown eyes, though one of them looks a little strange. You may have noticed his hands—very artistic and manicured."

The young woman blinked.

Fortunately there was hardly any traffic just then in that part of the terminal. The agents at the neighboring counters could hear me perfectly, which proved an unexpected boon.

"You are inquiring about the harp?" came a voice from the USAir counter.

I turned toward the voice. The young woman, scarcely out of her teens, was rather short with a round face and what appeared to be natural curls all over her head. A plastic tag on her jacket said she was Jacqueline Rose.

"I have tried and tried to contact Mr. García," she said. "You can tell him that the harp arrived safely and is being held for him in the Madrid airport."

Yes, it would be a harp—those calluses on the finger-tips—obviously my man!

I moved over to the USAir desk.

"Thank heavens! I said. "I am a Pink Lady at the hospital. Mr. García was admitted unconcious and without identification. Since he seemed to mumble something about flights and luggage, I was asked to come here on the chance that some-one might remember him." My story was very flimsy, and of course I would not have known about his eyes if he had been unconcious, but that's neither here nor there.

Miss Rose looked as though she might be truly concerned.

I asked, "Can you give me any further information about Mr.—I believe you said García?"

"Just a minute," she answered and walked over to a com-puter into which she began to type something. As she waited for the computer to reply, she said: "That certainly explains why I couldn't get hold of him. I tried three times, at his motel—the Sunset. The last time I called, they told me he had checked out. He was to leave Sunday morning, the twen-tieth."

I thought I had better talk fast before Miss Rose could gather her wits and begin to look at me curiously. I said, "He has not fully come to since he has been in the hospital, but there are times when he seems to be mumbling 'Berlin.' Do you have anything there that would indicate what his plans were?"

"Let me see." Miss Rose returned to the computer and

communed with it a short time. "Yes," she said, "he had a
reservation for Kennedy."

"When was that?"

"February twenty-first at ten-thirty-five."

At this point a phone rang. Miss Rose took it up and
hooked it under her chin. It was one of those conversations
in which the other party is off and on the line for some reason
or other. In one of the lulls, Miss Rose pulled a sheaf of notes
from under the counter and riffled through them. There was
a flash of pink fingernails as she covered the transmitter.
"Here's a note about the harp. You can look at it if you like."

There it was: Luís García Valera—Santa Barbara to San
Francisco to Dallas–Fort Worth to Charlotte to Three City
Airport. And from Three City to Kennedy and from
Kennedy to Spain.

"On what date to Spain?" I wondered aloud.

A young man entered the booth. Miss Rose, still holding
the phone and waiting for the return of her party, said, "Bill,
do you remember a no-show on García one day last week?"

The young man turned the baggage ticket he was holding
and made a notation on the back of it. "García? García?" he
mumbled vaguely as he made a feeble effort to recall.

"You remember," Miss Rose prompted, "The gentleman—you know—in the green suede jacket." She rolled her
eyes in exaggeration. "The one we had so much trouble
tracing the harp for."

"That one!" the young man answered. "There was a no-
show—might have been him—on Tuesday."

"It would have been a no-show on Sunday," Miss Rose
corrected. She completed the telephone conversation and
returned to the computer. García's flight to Madrid was supposed to have been on the twenty-first. "Uh, yes," she said,
"I remember that jacket. For an older gentleman, Mr. García
was downright sexy looking. His clothes were tough, but on

him they looked good—and I say if an old man can do it, why not?"

I was a bit taken aback. The man in question was very little if any older than I. But whether or not the man was valiantly fighting old age with a toupee and a green jacket, he was clearly the man whose body we had found at Brown Spring.

Those sensitive hands—of course! They could only have belonged to a musician. And with the toupee and "tough" clothing, he might well have been sexy with that glorious glow of the sun on his skin. Perhaps I would have thought him so myself; and the girls in the chapter would have agreed, no doubt. I wanted to ask about his hair (that is, the toupee), but I didn't dare.

"I can't thank you enough," I said—in as gracious a manner as I could muster, hoping to make up for my earlier behavior.

Luís García Valera—a Spanish harpist—expected in Madrid, left from Santa Barbara.

Was he on a concert tour? Possibly the last concert of the tour was in Santa Barbara. Why had nobody in Madrid asked why he didn't show up? And why had he come to Borderville?

As I was thinking of these things, my eye lighted on the Rentz Auto Rental sign: THE DEPENDABLE AUTOMOBILE RENTAL SERVICE—FOR LESS! as the television ads are always reminding us. Since I was at the airport anyhow, I might as well see if García had rented a car. So I walked over to their office and asked.

He had. It had been driven back some time in the dark hours of Monday morning the twenty-first and left in front of the office. It had been driven fifty-seven miles. I told the young man in the office that García had given me a check that had bounced. I asked for a description of García. The young man's description tallied with that of Miss Rose. I asked him especially about the jacket.

"It was strictly neat-o," he replied, "very cool." From the young man's language I took it that my informant knew what he was talking about.

I asked for the young man's name (he was Brent Millmarsh) and left.

Hubris? Sophocles never portrayed it any more effectively. I had a feeling that I had just pulled off a marvelously effective escapade and the whole world had better get out of my way before I knocked it over. I was like a cat that has eaten a mockingbird. There I was—fifty-seven years old with two grown children (and very attractive, straight young people even if I did rear them myself), married to a highly respected and occasionally stuffy attorney—and telling lies all over the Three City Airport!

Meddlesome! That's what my grandmother would have called it. But I had been successful. And it felt grand. As soon as I got home, I went straight to the telephone and rang the sheriff's office; and then when Butch Gilroy came on the line, I said, "Mr. Gilroy, this is Helen Delaporte."

Perhaps I ought to explain that during the time Calvin Gilroy has been sheriff of Ambrose County, my Henry has made a fool of him on the witness stand more than once. Butch Gilroy has no reason to like either of us.

So there was a little pause while Butch sucked in his breath. "All right, Helen, what have you got?"

He has no excuse for calling me Helen. All the world calls him Butch, but I have never called him anything but "Mr. Gilroy"—to his face, that is.

"I have the name of that so-called bum my ladies found at Brown Spring, and he's no bum at all, but an internationally known musician."

That is the sort of thing hubris will do to a girl. If I had begun that communication in the right way—meek tone, uncertain manner—if I had been the stupid female with no idea what to do with some little thing I had just happened to notice, he would have put it together, claimed it for himself, and been a self-made hero. But no. In one sentence I had signaled that I was a cantankerous female who can do his job better than he can.

There was silence on the other end of the line to the count of five.

"Is that so?" he said at last.

"Indeed it is," I chirped. "His name is Luís García Valera. He is Spanish and a most accomplished harpist."

"A what?"

"Harpist—he plays the harp."

"And how did he get himself killed by a wino in Brown Spring Cemetery?" The tone was resonant with sarcasm.

"It's your business to find that out."

"Fine," said our fearless law-enforcer, "I'll do that."

I got the message immediately: I had just received the brush-off.

"You don't understand," I said. I was going on the defensive now, which is the wrong thing to do. "His name is García," I protested. "They told me so at the airport. There is no possible doubt about it."

"Listen, Helen," Gilroy broke in, "we're very busy here today. We'll take care of this just as soon as we get around to it. Okay?"

I was mad and chagrined. Because I was excited, I had acted like a child, and I had been treated like a child. But I did not lick my wounds. I immediately called the commonwealth attorney, Ronald Jefferson.

Ron is no special favorite of mine, but he belongs to the country club and has played golf with Henry once or twice. And his wife, of course, is in Lawyers' Wives, a funny little club that meets for cocktails once a year. Ron is not smart like Henry, and Henry says he is lazy but honest. He is pretty;

that's how he gets elected. He is also smooth. And that's all he is.

"Ron," I said when the young woman put me through to him, "this is Helen Delaporte."

"Ah, Helen! This makes my day."

I could picture him in his big paneled office with a cigar in his left hand and that huge gold ring he wears—with a crest on it—totally fake, of course. That's one thing you learn quickly in the DAR.

"Good to hear from you, doll! Anything I can do, just ask."

I began at the beginning. I told Ron the whole thing. He kept murmuring such things as "Now isn't that amazing!" and "Well, well!" After I had told my whole story and given him the names of Rose and Millmarsh, he said, "Well, dear, you've really given us something to think about. Yes, indeed! Something to think about."

There was a pause. Then I heard his swivel chair squeak as he took his feet off the desk.

"Have you got those names?" I asked.

"Oh yes—er—Rose and Middlemarch."

"The second name is Millmarsh." And I spelled it for him.

"Ross and Millmarsh," he repeated. "Well, I'll tell you what, dear; we'll check this out and get back to you, right?"

What can be said to something like that? What I said was, "I would certainly appreciate it if you would." I knew what his words meant and I knew what *he* meant; and they weren't the same thing.

"Bye-bye, now," he purred, and put the phone in its cradle. I sat there with a dead instrument in my hand. Ron Jefferson, unlike Gilroy, had given me the *velvet* brush-off. While I was still holding the phone in my hand, I heard a click. Ron had picked up his phone again. He was trying to call out. It didn't work. I sat holding my own instrument waiting to see what would happen. In less than a minute there was a click again, and I heard, "Oh, Goddamn it." I hung up.

I just sat there in the breakfast room looking at the amaryllis that was trying to bloom. Ron Jefferson was no doubt talking to Butch Gilroy by this time. And no doubt they were talking about me. I could very easily imagine what they were saying. But it wouldn't be flattering—I was sure of that.

I made considerable progress with the music for Holy Week. Saint Luke's is not especially high; but though it is a small parish, quite a number of our people are knowledgeable and can tell good music from bad. Not that they know how much it takes to produce good music. Few of them have any idea what it's like to play for that long service on Palm Sunday, three hours on Good Friday, the Easter Vigil, and then Easter morning. When the vocal music is added, an organist–choir director has enough to occupy her in February and March without the DAR, and certainly without a murder.

Henry came in at 6:45. He had been in court all day and was tired. I got out two fillets and frozen peas and put some potatoes on and mashed them. It's his favorite meal! There were two slices of lemon pie left. That and two cups of coffee seemed to revive him.

Over the last cup I told him about my day. He did not seem surprised. He pulled his chin and looked out the window at the oldest Blankenbeckler boy across the street revving up his Honda under the streetlight.

"Well," Henry said, "you definitely have important information there. You've got a name, and it's the name of a missing man, whether it turns out to be the murdered man or not. If Butch wants to trace this García, he'll easily find out the truth of the matter. If García was in town any length of time, his movements should not be hard to discover. He must have cashed travelers' checks and shown proof of identity more than once. Butch can do a lot with that if he wants to.

"But what you'll have to prove to Butch is that the man who flew in to Three City Airport is the same man who was found at the Brown Spring Cemetery, and he'll resist the proof.

"It was a stroke of luck that what's-his-name made such a thing about his harp."

"García Valera," I interjected.

"García Valera," Henry repeated. "Butch will check the motel and make further inquiries at the airport. Apparently you gave a pretty accurate description. All of that from looking at a battered corpse for a few minutes! I have a very intelligent wife. You would make a good witness. Perhaps I can use you sometime."

Although Henry was teasing, I liked it.

"Of course," Henry continued, "there will have to be a positive identification by someone who knew García. Butch is going to resist your identification."

"Why?"

"Natural inertia. A man comes here traveling under the name of García. Well enough! But nobody has missed him. If this is García, you would think someone would wonder why he hasn't showed up wherever he was expected to be. Consider the harp. People don't carry them around unless they are going to play them somewhere. So why hasn't García been missed? And why hasn't there been an outcry? And where is his luggage other than the harp?

"You and I are pretty sure that García, the man at the airport, was also the man you found at Brown Spring last Wednesday. But Butch will have to find someone who knew him and have the body identified."

The following day I went on with the housecleaning. I got all the mildew off the shower curtains in the downstairs bathroom and reorganized the shelves in the pantry. I divided and repotted the shamrocks. In fact I kept so busy that I didn't even practice.

I cooked a nice pot roast and made a congealed salad. We

enjoyed both; and by the time I had the dinner dishes put away, I had no intention of doing one other thing or having a serious thought. I propped myself up with pillows and read a detective story until Henry came to bed.

In the morning, as usual, Henry took the first section of the *Banner-Democrat* while I read the grocery ads. My idea of sexual equality is to have two subscriptions to the *Banner-Democrat* so that I do not have to wait for the first section. But since Henry goes out and finds the paper where it is so often thrown—under the holly hedge—it is only right that he should get the first section if he wants it.

He reads absolutely every word on the editorial page, then swaps it for the financial page, and thus gets through his juice, cereal, toast, and eggs most days without a word.

On the other hand, it is very pleasant after he has left for the office. I pour a second cup of coffee and sit there in my robe leisurely scanning the front page, the obituaries, the features (I always read "Dear Abby," although I can't stand the woman). Then there is the club calendar.

I had got that far when my eye lighted on the following story:

DAR CORPSE STILL NOT IDENTIFIED

No evidence has been found to identify the body of an apparent derelict discovered last week by a party of local DARs in a rural cemetery in Ambrose County. Sheriff Calvin ("Butch") Gilroy observed that identity can be established only if the body can be identified by a relative or associate unless the deceased's fingerprints are on file.

"Those transients give us lots of trouble," Gilroy said, "but we're working on it."

The body was discovered last Tuesday by
members of the Old Orchard Fort Chapter,
NSDAR, in search of the grave of Adoniram
Philipson, soldier of the American Revolution.
Mrs. Henry Delaporte, Regent of the chapter,
led a committee charged with the project of
memorializing the long-dead hero.

The story went on from there—about five more inches.

My first reaction was surprise that the form was exactly
right: "Old Orchard Fort Chapter, NSDAR. *DAR* is correct
too, but *NSDAR*, which stands for National Society Daughters of the American Revolution, is better. That seems so
simple, but it is surprising how often the papers get it wrong.
I had not yet learned, you see, of Elizabeth's educational
campaign.

Although glad to see the story because of course it would
count as inches, written as it was, I hardly had time to be
pleased before I realized that the news story proved that Butch
Gilroy had absolutely ignored me—just as I had suspected.

I picked up the phone and called the *Banner-Democrat*.
They put me through to Albert Manley, whom I did not at
that point know, although I got to know him and like him
very much later on. I told Al how I had identified the dead
man and had notified both Gilroy and Jefferson.

Al perked up right away; and if I had only realized it, I had
just ensured myself a degree of notoriety. But I was so provoked by that stupid sheriff that I didn't much care what I was
doing.

After I finished my conversation with Al Manley, I rang the
sheriff's office.

"Sheriff Gilroy?" I said when he came on the phone. He
recognized my voice.

"Now, Helen, you had a nice little time being detective.

But you know we in the sheriff's department are profession-
als. We have experience in these things and procedures that
we follow. Amateurs don't know anything about procedures,
and so they make mistakes."

"What are you talking about?" I demanded. "I identified
that corpse for you. You were hardly civil when I gave you
the information. I also gave all the evidence to Ron Jefferson.
There is no doubt that the man was Luís García Valera. Now
what do you mean by telling the *Banner-Democrat* that no
identification has been made?"

"Now we investigated thoroughly at the Sunset Inn. Valera was there all right—but he checked out. And we made a
special inquiry at the airport. And what do you know—
Valera went out on USAir Flight four-oh-seven on Sunday
morning to New York."

"Did what?"

"Left town about eighteen hours after the coroner says that
bum you stumbled onto out there at Brown Spring had
already turned in his chips. Like I say, we use procedures. We
check everything. We know what we are doing. We use
standard procedures."

"Too bad you don't use your brain."

"Don't what?"

"Use your brain. I told you that girl at the ticket desk
recognized Mr. García immediately from my description."

"Well, of course!" Butch said. "It was this Valera guy; but
like I told you, he got on a plane and went to New York."

"How could he get on a plane and go to New York when
he was lying dead in the Brown Spring Cemetery?" I demanded.

"But he wasn't lying dead in the Brown Spring Cemetery," Butch insisted. "That was somebody else—like I
say—a bum."

"Look," I said, "I saw the man's body. I described him

accurately, and that Miss Rose recognized the description immediately. You can't tell me that Luís García Valera had a doppelgänger lying dead in the cemetery while the real García flew off to New York."

"Had a what?"

"Doppelgänger—an exact double."

"Well, he must have had one of those things, because it's a cinch he flew to New York on USAir Flight four-oh-seven."

What do you say to a person like that? I just said, "I am going to say good-bye to you, Sheriff Gilroy. But I'm warning you that you are going to hear from me again."

"Suit yourself."

I felt that I absolutely had to do something about the situation immediately. And so I called Henry, but Henry was in court. So I tried to get Al Manley again. Al had also gone to the courthouse. (There was a big liability suit against the city that the whole town had been following, and it was about to come to a decision.)

Then I calmed down a bit and began to do some constructive thinking. I reviewed a few things. The man named Luís García Valera had come in on USAir Flight 326, and he had had a reservation also on USAir. He had come to Borderville from Santa Barbara on the way to New York.

Santa Barbara! Ethel Muehlbach! Wasn't that where Ethel lives? Of course it was!

I met Ethel at Continental Congress three years ago and then happened to run into her again in Constitution Hall last year when I was in Washington with Henry.

Mills graduate—and a very smart girl. And it seemed to me that her husband is a surgeon. She is the kind of girl who would know about any major event in Santa Barbara. I looked at my watch. It was ten o'clock. Maybe at 1:30 it would be safe to call her.

I had plenty to do in the meantime. I never get all the Christmas cards addressed on time, and that means I have to write letters to all the people who didn't get the card. The result is that my friends from the latter part of the alphabet expect long letters from me in January and February. But I was down to the *W*s. I was doing pretty well for me.

In fact 1:30 arrived just about the time I realized I was hungry. I made up half a package of Knorr soup and had some of the leftover congealed salad. And that was lunch.

I got Ethel's number from the directory service. She picked up the phone on the third ring.

"Helen!" she squealed when I said my name and did my song-and-dance about Continental Congress. "Of course I remember you. Where are you?"

In some ways it was better in the old days when the operator used to announce: "You have a long-distance call from Phoenix, Arizona," or wherever. You knew it was long distance then, but now I had to explain that I was in Borderville; and again she said, "Where?"

We are not a famous town, but we are not insignificant either. We have approximately thirty thousand people on the Tennessee side and almost forty thousand on the Virginia side. Parsons City, seventeen miles south of us, has eighty-five thousand and a large regional university; and Cooksport, the other point on our triangle, is twenty-five miles away with seventy-five thousand. So we are not a mere hamlet, and the three cities with their shared airport form a center for light industry, trade, and transportation. But the world does not know this, and I am constantly having to explain. For present purposes I contented myself by stating that I was calling from Tennessee.

I asked Ethel if Luís García Velera had given a concert in Santa Barbara.

"Lu García?"

"Luís García Valera," I repeated.

"We call him Lu. Of course I've heard him many times. He's awfully good. I suppose you are thinking of him for your concert series."

"He lived there in Santa Barbara!"

"Why yes, he does."

So García's home was Santa Barbara, and he was taking his harp to Spain but had made a side trip to Borderville, Virginia-Tennessee, a place that some people believed, albeit erroneously, to be out of the way.

"Suppose you just tell me all you know about him," I said.

"Oh," Ethel began, "he's a very nice man. Arthur knows him—plays golf with him now and then and of course he belongs to the club. His wife was very nice—southern girl—died suddenly about eight years ago—very sad!

"He's highly regarded as a musician and has his own conservatory—the García School, I think he calls it. People come from just about everywhere to study harp with him. The harp is such a beautiful instrument—let me see . . ."

There was a pause before Ethel went on. "I read—that's it—he's gone abroad, concert tour. Oh, he's just very fine."

"Ethel," I said, "are you where you are comfortable?"

"Yes," she said, "Why?"

"Good, because I have a long story, and you'll find it interesting." I told her about the whole adventure and my problems with Butch Gilroy.

"You don't mean it!" she said when I had finished. "But then I have always said that a Regent, if she is worth anything, can handle any crisis, and you are a Regent. Now what can I do to help you?"

"You've already done a lot," I replied. "But suppose you give me a description."

"He's very good looking," she said. "Maybe sixty or more. His parents were refugees—perhaps came to America about thirty-six. Yes, I'd say he is at least sixty—dark, of course—lots of wavy hair."

"Could it be a wig?" I interrupted.

Ethel laughed. "Yes, it is. Much too good to be true. Well, let's see—I would say the features are regular. Rather heavy eyebrows. Rimless spectacles. Not quite six feet tall. Medium build—very expensive clothes—always. His wife had money."

"Does he have relatives there?"

"No—none here, I think. I could ask."

"Do," I said, "and I can't thank you enough."

As soon as we disconnected, I knew what I had to do. I was positive that the person who used García's ticket on USAir had not been García. I was going to build a fire under Butch Gilroy and make him do the right thing. I immediately called Al Manley at the *Banner-Democrat* and told him I was absolutely sure that the corpse in question was Luís García Valera of the García School of Music in Santa Barbara, California, that he was known internationally, and that efforts were being made through a friend to locate the next of kin.

I explained that I knew Ethel through the DAR. He kept asking me specific questions, and I hardly knew whether I should pull back before plunging into such notoriety as the *Banner-Democrat* could create. But I went right ahead.

The next morning I read the following story:

DAR IDENTIFIES BODY

Transcontinental Cooperation of Women's
Organization Provides Information

The body discovered ten days ago by representatives of the Old Orchard Fort Chapter, DAR, of Borderville has now been identified as that of the internationally known musician and

educator Luís García Valera, according to Mrs.
Henry Delaporte, Regent of the chapter.

A clue picked up at Three City Airport led to
Santa Barbara, California, where Delaporte
contacted DAR member Ethel Muehlbach.
Through Muehlbach an accurate description of
García was secured. "The body we found in
Brown Spring Cemetery tallied in every way
with the description furnished by Mrs. Muehlbach," Delaporte stated. "I have not the slight-
est doubt that the man buried as a pauper here
last week was in reality a musician of interna-
tional reputation," she added.

Delaporte and Muehlbach became ac-
quainted when both were delegates in 1983 to
Continental Congress, an annual meeting at
the national headquarters of the DAR in Washington.

"She was quite surprised when I contacted
her," Delaporte said of the Santa Barbara
woman. It is not unusual, she observed, for
delegates to Continental Congress to meet and
form friendships with delegates from widely
separated chapters. "I have met many interesting
women through the DAR, but I never expected
one of them to help me identify a corpse,"
Delaporte said.

There was also a story headed SHERIFF TERMS IDENTITY
PREPOSTEROUS. And of course Butch Gilroy was contending
that García Valera had boarded a plane to Kennedy that
Sunday.

HOW THE PUBLICITY
BEGAN TO SPREAD

Elizabeth Wheeler

Mr. Manley was so nice and checked every DAR story with me to be sure he had written it right, and the story in the *Banner-Democrat* had all the details right so that we could get our credit for the inches. I just went right into the kitchen and got busy.

Now, I promised that young man some Belgrade bread. That's a recipe that I have never seen in any of the books. I got it from one of Mama's friends—she was Austrian—and she was an old lady forty years ago, so it is an old recipe going way, way back. Anyhow, it is just one of the best cookie recipes I know anything about. Here's how you make it:

BELGRADE BREAD

Cream 5 eggs and 2 cups sugar. Add 4 oz. finely cut or ground almonds, 1 t. nutmeg, ¼ t. cloves, 1 t. baking powder, 4 oz. citron finely

cut. Then add 3 to 4 cups flour to make a stiff
batter. Roll out to thickness of ¼ in. and cut
into desired shapes. Paint top of each cookie
with beaten whole egg to which a little milk
may be added. Bake in 350° oven 8 to 10 minutes. They should not be baked too long because they become hard.

So that was the recipe I made; and I put the cookies in a
nice box, prettied myself up, and went down to the newspaper office. And there was Mr. Manley; he said he had been
expecting me. I told him he could always count on me and
that I was sure I could count on him.

He just opened up the box and started in, and all the other
people in the office had learned what to expect whenever I
came in; and they came over right away. So I guess I didn't
make too many cookies after all.

We had just a wonderful time, and I liked the other reporters and secretaries and so on just as much as I liked Mr.
Manley. I don't know whether they liked me, but I must say
that they liked my Belgrade bread. Then Mr. Manley said,
"You know, I put that story on the wire."

I didn't really know what that meant.

"I sent it out on the wire," he said. "It will go to the
Associated Press."

I guess my eyes must have got big about that time, because
he said, "Oh, not all the papers will print it, but some will,
and you'll get lots of inches."

My! I never expected anything like that, and I began to
think what I could do for that nice young man. So I promised
him I would keep the goodies coming just as long as he did
the right thing by the DAR. And he said, "I think we can do
business. That sort of makes us partners, doesn't it?"

I said, "It sure does."

As I was going out, he said, "I'll be on the lookout for the story in the exchange." That's the papers in other towns that exchange with the *Banner-Democrat*.

About three days later, the mail began to come in. Friends from all over east Tennessee and Virginia and Kentucky and North Carolina and West Virginia began sending clippings to our members. We got clippings from Roanoke, Marion, Parsons City, Cooksport, Knoxville—just everywhere. And Alice Turner's niece saw the story and sent it to us from Indianapolis! When we got all the clippings together, we had almost two yards of publicity; and I felt sure it would all count because it was about our chapter and our project and all.

IDENTIFYING THE BODY
OF LUÍS GARCÍA

Hornsby Roadhever

I am writing this at the request of Mrs. Helen Delaporte, who as I understand it intends to include it in the minutes of her DAR chapter.

I am Hornsby Roadheaver of the Roadheaver Agency in San Francisco. I manage between fifty and sixty of the biggest names in music and dance on the West Coast. I book my artists with the Community Series Inc. and with all the big symphonies and civic opera companies in the United States and Canada. Lately I have booked several concert tours in Europe.

I began handling Luís García seventeen years ago. Since that time he has averaged about ten concerts a year. Over the years he has made in the neighborhood of $180,000 with me, and I don't have to tell you it has been profitable for me also.

Lu was a different sort of fellow. You could say that about any of my artists, but Lu was not only different from ordinary people, he was different from other artists. I would say he was proud—not proud in the same way all artists are, but proud in his own way.

You take a soprano who has a few notes above high C. There is something about that that she just can't get over. Every third sentence she speaks for the rest of her life will have something about "my career" in it. She can't find anything good to say about any other soprano, unless she is being interviewed on TV—but that's another matter.

You never saw a man as polite as Lu was. There was no respect he demanded for himself that he didn't show to other people. Dapper—good looking in a way—he was just something you don't run into except in old novels—maybe like *The Count of Monte Cristo*—I think that's the title of it.

You would never say I was close to Lu—nobody was—but we've had dinner, cocktails, whatever else together for all those years. He was always friendly. But in spite of that, we never quite managed to become real friends—you know.

Still, I liked the guy; and when I read that he had passed away, well, just thinking of the guy himself, the first thought that came to me was: "I'm sorry. Something important got away from me again. It was too bad I hadn't known him better." It wasn't till a couple days later that I thought about how much money I was kissing good-bye.

But after all, our relationship had been business; and even though he was now dead, the business was unfinished. There was an agent in Madrid who would be getting nervous, and he would be screaming pretty soon because Lu did not show up.

You see, what Lu had planned to do was to take rooms in Madrid, where he could rest up and practice before he began the tour.

So there would be no reason for me or anyone else to miss Lu (he had no family here) until almost time for his first concert.

It was a real shock to learn from the morning paper that one of my very own artists had been murdered.

It took me about an hour to realize that it was up to *me* to do something about it. You see, he lived down there in Santa Barbara. I knew he didn't have any family, and I didn't have the ghost of an idea who his lawyer was or his accountant. He had a little school down there—just his own—just harp and nothing else.

But you see, I had that number, and I called it.

The voice that belonged to the second in command down there sounded very sweet and very young to me. "Dear," I said, "how old are you?"

"What is this?" The voice didn't sound quite so sweet anymore.

"Well," I said, "if you are forty-five, I have an unpleasant task to dump on you: notifying some people in Europe that since they are not going to be seeing Lu García after all, they had better send his baggage back and who knows what else (I never had an artist die like this before); but if you are under twenty-four, I'll do it myself."

"I'm twenty-six," she said.

"I think I'll do it for you anyhow."

"Is it about the Spanish tour?"

"Yes."

There was one of those pregnant pauses we so often read about.

Then I said I was Hornsby Roadheaver; and yes, she knew who I was. And she knew that Lu had sent his harp and all his luggage except for one bag direct to an address in Calle Calderon in Madrid. She sounded really forlorn.

"Were you close to him?" I asked.

"Not in that way," she replied. "He was just a wonderful man, and he taught me everything I know." She sounded like she really meant it, and I was afraid she was going to cry into the phone just any second.

"Do you know any more about—" I began. "Do you know any more about what happened?"

"No, only what's in the paper just now."

Can you imagine it! The poor kid didn't know anything about it until she saw it in the paper. And here I had been smart-mouthing all over the wire.

Well, I could see that this sweet kid didn't know anything that I didn't know. But I had the news story in front of me—all about the DAR, if you would believe it! "Dear, I tell you what," I said. "Just look up the number of this Ethel Muehlbach for me, and I'll let you go."

I could hear the pages rustle as she looked up the listing in the book. When I got the number, I thanked her and rang off.

And that was how I got to know Janie Sieburg—because that's who that sweet voice belongs to, and there's more to be said about her in a later installment.

Muehlbach gave me Helen Delaporte's number. I called Helen right away, and she was the other good thing that happened to me that day. Janie and Helen are two real charmers in very different ways. Janie—the young chick—a knockout to look at, as I soon found out (but an excellent harpist and I am going to get her engagements and she will pack the houses as soon as the public sees her picture), real blond hair and gentian eyes. And just wait until they hear her play. And Helen—mature, poised, intellectual, forceful. And when I got to know her, I found out that she is an excellent musician too and dedicated to her work.

I rang up Helen immediately and explained who I was.

"I guess you are sure this man was Lu García?" I said.

"Without question," she came back. I knew from the way she said it that she was right. But you know how sometimes you just hope that what you know is true isn't that way after all.

"Could you just describe him a little?" I said.

She told me all the usual things—height, weight, age, etc. And then she said there was something strange about the appearance of the left eye. You see, that was one of the few things he told me of a personal nature about himself. He didn't use the word *blind,* but he said that with monovision he did not like driving more than was necessary.

Then she asked me about his hair. I said that he had a regular forest on his head. The fact is I often envied him because my own crop is getting a little sparse up there.

She said that was a discrepancy, but she felt sure that there was a wig missing. So—I was willing to buy that, because that hair of his really looked like an ad for Breck.

Then she went on with the description, and it checked out right along. When she came to the clothes he had on in the air terminal, I knew there couldn't be any mistake because of the suede jacket. That just sounded like Lu García: flash, but class just the same. From the description, it had to be Lu.

Then Helen told me about some man who used Lu's name and flew out of that Three City Airport on Sunday after Lu would seem to have been killed.

I was getting to be a little puzzled. I was searching around in my mind for something, and I wasn't sure what that might be. But I had told that cute voice down in Santa Barbara that I would do a job for her.

I needn't have worried about what to do because Helen told me what it was.

"Take down this number," she said. It was the number of the commonwealth attorney. "The best thing to do is call him," she said. "They are not going to do a thing at this end as long as they can deny the identity. But if you call Ron

Jefferson and demand clarification, the next move will have to be his."

So Helen and I hung up, and I dialed that commonwealth attorney and just barely caught him in the office because by that time it was almost five o'clock there in the East. I offered to send him publicity stills for identification, but he said the only way to identify the body was for someone who knew Lu to look at the corpse.

Now, I really wasn't interested in a transcontinental flight to some place called Borderville in the Virginia boondocks. I mean, after all, even though my Daddy was on the Bible-Belt revival circuit for years, I don't manage country and western. I was very dubious. He said I should let him know if I was going to make the trip so he could get an exhumation order. It really didn't sound like a party I wanted to attend.

After we rang off, I got to thinking about it. I was in the soup on this anyhow I looked at it. I dithered about it all evening and finally called Janie again the next morning. We did considerable talking before I asked for the name and number of Lu's lawyer, which was why I called her in the first place.

The lawyer said that there would be trouble with the estate unless we could get a death certificate for Lu García and, what's more, that Janie was the biggest beneficiary of his will.

After that second talk with Janie, I was ready to do just about anything to look like Mr. Big to her. So I thought maybe I would go back there to Borderville and identify the remains. All the same, it looked to me like the round-trip ticket would be just a little pricey. But then I asked this lawyer if the trip might be charged to the estate. As soon as he said yes, my mind was made up that I was going to take a trip east.

So I went to Borderville.

I got to Three City Airport at 11:45 P.M. on Sunday, March 6, because I missed a connection at a place called

Charlotte, North Carolina. I checked in at the Sunset Inn just next to the terminal at Three City and didn't wake up the next morning until half past ten. I called this Jefferson person—the commonwealth attorney. He sounded relieved to hear from me because he had the undertaker ready to dig up the coffin. He told me he would send a car for me at two o'clock.

As soon as I looked out, I saw mountains; and believe me, it was cold outside with heavy clouds. I got in the car beside the driver and began to wish I hadn't. The roads were like absolutely drunk, and this guy's driving was like something else.

We finally pulled into a cemetery and drove clear to the back, which seemed to be where they plant paupers and such.

The grave had already been opened, and the coffin all crudded up with red clay was on the surface at one side. Jefferson shook my hand, said he was glad to see me, and asked how it was at the Sunset Inn, then told the undertaker's man to open her up.

It was worse than I expected. The lower part of Lu's face looked like it had been tenderized. His nose was smashed in, and the undertaker hadn't bothered to rebuild anything.

There was no hair topside, but the suntan came right up to the line and the scalp was strictly pale skin from there on. The face was in really bad condition, and he had been dead for some time, but I knew in my vitals that this was Lu García.

I nodded, "That's him."

The D.A. turned to the undertaker and said, "Take him to the morgue. I suppose the body is to be sent to California?"

"Yes," I said, though I hadn't thought of it before. I sure hoped that somebody would do something to make Lu look better before Janie saw him.

There were some papers for me to sign.

"When does your plane leave?"

"Four-thirty," I said.

"Where would you like us to take you?"

"Sunset Inn," I said, and he told the driver to take me there.

Going back out that hilly road, I guess I was a little reflective, the way you are after a funeral. Lu and I had been friendly—a glass of wine, a good steak, that kind of thing. He had a real talent, and I was pretty depressed that it had come to this. In fact I didn't realize for about ten minutes that it had begun to snow in a sort of neglectful way.

By the time we got to the inn, the snow had got down to business. It had been a long time since I was in a real snowstorm. About three-thirty I opened my door and stood under the overhang just a minute. The snow was two and a half inches on the ground and there was not a sound. I looked over toward the control tower. As I thought about it, I hadn't heard a plane come in for half an hour. I called the ticket counter. All flights canceled. There I was without even an *Esquire*. I had already found out that the TV in my room was one that Noah threw out of the ark. What to do? Then I happened to think that I had had that telephone contact with Helen Delaporte. I decided to give her a call.

That turned out to be a smart move, because she came out and got me—through snow and ice—and gave me a big dinner that you couldn't buy at a San Francisco restaurant and entertained me like a movie star.

I finally flew out of Three City Airport at 3:00 the following afternoon.

WHO LUÍS GARCÍA VALERA
REALLY WAS

Helen Delaporte

Down here in the South, people don't consider that they
know a person until they know what his family is. Your
family is who you are. It's cozy, and it's an attitude that makes
it easier for a lot of women in this region to get into the DAR.
But more of that shortly.

That was quite a storm we showed Hornsby Roadheaver.
But it meant that we got to know him, and through him we
had finally got official recognition of García's identity. Although Roadheaver was not the type, he had studied for a
year at Juilliard; and he knew Julia and Mac Chapman. He
also managed Rachel Gillfallon, a flutist whom I knew at
Eastman.

Actually, when I said good-bye to Hornsby at Three City,
I thought the DAR part of the DAR mystery was over.

Of course I was mistaken. The headlines of the next morning read DAR REGENT RIGHT ABOUT MURDER. Then there was
a ream about me and the chapter, all of it a recap of what had

already been printed. At that point I had not yet found out that Elizabeth Wheeler had been bribing the newspaper for publicity. Of course every scrap of publicity we got in that manner was tweaking the nose of Butch Gilroy, not to mention Ron Jefferson.

I was immediately the town celebrity, and as soon as the telephone rates went down that evening, I found that I was a big hit with the Daughters all over the Commonwealth of Virginia.

"We're proud of you, Helen," the State Regent assured me. Actually, I was a little nervous because National is very touchy if we don't live up to their standards of dignity. For example, there are rules as to where we can and can't wear the DAR insignia. And there is a general atmosphere that, if not defensive, is at least cautious. And all the media are only too glad to ridicule us if we do anything in the least silly.

I got calls from Tazewell, Roanoke, Bedford—just everywhere.

Mabel Hazelhurst from the Royal Oak Chapter said, "Now, dear, you must go right ahead and solve that mystery."

She seemed to be serious about it, but I had no idea at all that our chapter would become further involved.

Nevertheless we did, and things began to stir the very next Sunday. Nearly everybody had left the church, and I was winding down the postlude when I looked up and saw Frances Vogelsang, who was on altar guild that month. Her round, bland face appeared above the console like a moon fifteen minutes above the horizon.

"I read about you," she cooed.

"I'm notorious."

"That Mr. García," she said, "he's the one that married Evelyn Haverty, isn't he?"

"Oh?" I was gathering up my music.

"Yes. Her mother was a Drover from Benhams."

I am generally accepted by the people in this area; nevertheless there are ways in which I am very much an outsider and always will be. Benhams I had heard of, but I had never been there. And as for Havertys, I had never heard of them. But the prospect of increasing my knowledge about the murdered man roused my interest.

"Evelyn Haverty, you say?"

"My sister Elaine, the one who lives in Knoxville, was in school with Dora Drover. Dora went out to California—oh, at least thirty-five years ago. I am just about sure that her daughter Evelyn married a man named García."

Frances Vogelsang's name pretty well describes her, and I never had thought that she was strong on brains, but people like that often know things that nobody else knows, and I have to hand it to them.

I went right home and called Elizabeth.

TRACING THE DROVER LINE FROM JACOB DROVER TO THE PRESENT

Elizabeth Wheeler

I had no idea that I was getting further mixed up in our famous "murder" when Helen Delaporte called me that Sunday afternoon. I thought at first she was calling about some lady wanting help with a DAR line. But this little project sounded a lot more exciting.

I am not *really* what you would call a professional genealogist, but I have always been interested in families. When I was just a little girl, I loved to listen to my grandmother and aunt Mattie as they would sit on the porch and talk about relatives for hours—not just our relatives, but the relatives of everybody in the little mountain town where we lived. Papa was the town doctor, and he used to go to all the hollows and across the ridges, and I soon learned that I had kinfolks in just about all those places. And those who weren't kin to me were kin to those who were.

Well, after I went off to school, I got interested in the history of Virginia. For most people that means Williamsburg and the Carters, Byrds, Lees, and Washingtons. But I was interested in Dr. Thomas Walker and Colonel Patton and Colonel William Preston and Madam Russell and the Over-Mountain Men.

And that's pretty much how I got my reputation for gene-alogy in southwest Virginia—just always trying to find out as much as I could about the past of the area where I grew up.

Now I had the problem of Evelyn Haverty. At first the name didn't mean a thing to me. Her mother was a Drover. Well, the hills are full of Drovers. Then it came to me that she must be part of the Quin Drover clan.

When I was a very small girl in Hogg's Gap, I remember seeing Quin and his nurse in a big old Pierce Arrow touring car. In those days he had to ship that car by rail to get it in and out of Hogg's Gap.

Quin lived up in New Jersey—which might have been China for all it meant to me—and just came to Hogg's Gap rarely.

His wife was buried in the Hogg's Gap Cemetery in a great huge granite mausoleum. And then when he died, they bur-ied him there too. That mausoleum was a show in itself, but I won't get off onto that.

When I run a genealogy, I go to the courthouse for the real evidence that I can use as proof. But first I try to find some-body who knows what the facts are, more or less, so I'll have something to start on.

This time I knew exactly where to go—Ella Fisk. Ella has lived in the mountains her whole life—almost ninety years now. After Wilber Fisk died leaving Ella with four little boys, she worked as district nurse for about fifty years. There's no creek in the hills that she doesn't know, and the miners and moonshiners think she is just about Mrs. God. She was bound to know about all those Drovers—the ones that were in the penitentiary as well as those who were out. I was pretty sure she would give me just what I needed.

My sister-in-law had been in the hospital for an operation the Wednesday before Helen Delaporte called me about the Drover genealogy. They took her home from the hospital the next Tuesday; so I had to go to Bluefield to be with her until she was able to take care of herself a little. I stayed with her ten days—which made me miss the DAR meeting—but on the way home I stopped by to see Ella Fisk and get everything she knew about the Drovers.

It is something to do to get to Ella's house. You go off the "big road" at Barnett's Chapel, and then you wind around up the hollow following automobile tracks till you come to a gate. After that it seems like a quarter of mile you have to walk before you get to the house.

It's the house where she was born. She lived in Hogg's Gap while she was district nurse—on account of the telephone, you know. But when she moved back to the home place, the boys had electricity and a telephone line put in. And I'd say that if Ella needed help, she could get it quick enough from folks that think the world of her—but that hollow is remote, and only a real mountain woman would think of living there.

It is a log house—a good, large-sized one—and the boys put a nice new roof on it. And she has a great high television thing up there.

I went trudging up the hollow in my overshoes, and it really takes lots of breath. I was right glad to see the smoke rolling out of her chimney, because the wind was whistling down the hollow, and in spite of the exercise, I was chilled all the way through.

Ella's boys all turned out well. One is a surgeon, one is a G.P.; one is a civil engineer, and the youngest—Douglass—is a high-school teacher in Grundy.

Doug has got the house fixed so that it is very comfortable and looks very nice.

It had been at least a year since I last saw Ellen, but she was the same as ever. She is quite a bit older than I am, but she used to work with Papa, and they just thought the world of each other. So if there was ever anybody like a big sister to me, it was Ella.

I explained what I was after.

"Quin Drover—" she said. "Yes, it was Quin, Jr., whose girl married the Haverty, and it seems to me her name was Dora. Yes, it was.

"You know, Quin, Jr., went to Emory and Henry College, and that's how he got to know Eudora Monahan. Her father was well-to-do in Benhams, and her brother was at Emory with Quin. I think she died when their only child was born. And so Quin gave her to Dora's mother to raise."

"Did he marry again?" I asked. When you are working on genealogy, you must always ask as many questions like that as you can.

"No—" Ella hesitated. "I don't believe he did. The daughter—her name was really Eudora—was just as well off being reared by the Monahans. And of course there was any amount of money ready for her."

I was trying to write all this down just as quick as Ellen said it. It's a good idea to keep an older person talking when you're asking for information, because once they begin remembering, there is no telling what you will learn.

"Now, was her father the one who used to come to Hogg's Gap in that great big Pierce Arrow?" I asked.

"No, no," Ella replied. "That was Quin, Sr."

"What do you know about him?"

"Know about him? I guess I know everything about him." Ella looked at me as if I had lost my senses. "Oh, you know all about him, don't you?"

I shook my head.

"Well," Ella said, "if you had as much to do with his poor relations as I have had, you'd know everything about him and a good deal more. He treated them like dirt, and they got even with him by telling every mean thing he ever did. But at the same time, they were proud to be related to him because he was rich; and they bragged about him at the same time that they hated him.''

Ella was a great help. If I hadn't had her, it would have taken months to do all the work that I did in just a week.

The first Drover in the mountains was Jacob Drover. He came to southwest Virginia soon after the Revolution with his wife, who was just Susan. Her maiden name is lost. He had twelve children—all of them sons. That's why the hills are so full of Drovers, although they were a quarrelsome lot and tended to get themselves shot early in life.

One of the sons was Andrew. He married Elizabeth Quinby. They say she was a shrewd, hard-driving woman; and though she had several children, the only one that had her brains was Quin Drover, Sr.

I later got his dates without any trouble right off the mausoleum in Hogg's Gap. He was born in 1840 and died in 1917. That made him just twenty-one years old when the War between the States broke out. Quin was wild and smart at the same time. Instead of going with the North or the South, he went with the bushwhackers. Soon he got to be their leader. He would go down toward Marion and just carry off everything he wanted from rich farmers and planters.

After the war had gone on quite a while, he saw which side would win. He went over into Kentucky and joined the Union army. By the time Lee surrendered, Quin Drover was a lieutenant.

When he got home, Quin knew how to steal, kill people, and make whiskey. But Quin was smart enough to make his whiskey the legal way, and he had enough money from his bushwhacking days to set up a still. He called the product Dixie Rose and began to get rich.

Quinby Drover, Sr., had five children; and the richer he

got, the higher they all got into society. After a while Quin got a bank. Then he got another one. Then he was principal stockholder in the R&HG railroad. After that he was just way above anybody else in the mountains. He got himself a private railway car and sent his boys to military schools and to college and his girls to finishing schools.

I've already mentioned Quin, Jr. Dora Monahan was a real beauty. She and Quin, Jr., were the grandparents of Evelyn Haverty, who was the one that married Luís García Valera. So that is how Mr. García Valera was related to the family.

Frank and Abner Drover went to Washington and Lee. Euphemia Bascomb was a friend of Frank's sister Martha at Laurel Hill College in Borderville. She came from a good family without money, but she was pretty and Frank married her. They lived in Washington until Frank died. Then Euphemia came back to live on the farm she had inherited from her father in Burke County; that's the one just below the Virginia border.

Frank and Euphemia had four children. The two older boys both died before they were twenty-five. St. Elmo was a broker like his father and committed suicide when he couldn't cover his commitments in 1929.

Their sister, Pearl Drover, married into a society family, but her husband never amounted to anything and was killed in an accident in '68, leaving one child: Bettye VanDyne.

Bettye VanDyne, then, was the only living descendant of Quin Drover, Jr.'s second son, and Ella thought Bettye was living on the old Bascomb place not far from Borderville.

I said, "Ella, how in the world do you know all this stuff?"

"Oh, the Drovers know all about it," she said.

Ella knew a great deal about Martha Drover's branch of the family; but there is no need to go into all the ins and outs of it (I've got it all written out in the chart) except to point out that Martha married Baker Comming—a lawyer for many years in Borderville and president of the Borderville State Bank that went under in 1932. After the bank failed, he ran the Drover and Sons Transfer and Storage until his son Allen came home from the war. Allen, Jr., took over when his father retired in 1967 and changed the name of the business to Borderville Transfer.

It's an interesting thing about Allen! There are still people around who blame the Commings for the bank failure.

Jane Drover married in Collinwood, New Jersey, where old Quin moved about 1900; and as you can see from the chart, there's only the one living descendant: Duncan Yardley. But there's a widower of Jane Drover's granddaughter: Dr. Anthony Hancock.

A. R. Drover, the last son of old Quin Drover, has a granddaughter still living—Dorothy. She grew up in the East. Kenneth Raebon was just a boy from Hogg's Gap who put himself through law school. Somehow he got to be attorney for the Drover interests in southwest Virginia (they had coal before it was all mined out) and met and married Dorothy. They live in Hogg's Gap.

So all told, there are only four direct descendants of old Quin Drover left. They are Bettye VanDyne, Allen Comming, Jr., Duncan Yardley, and Dorothy Raebon. In addition to these, Dr. Hancock is a grandson-in-law, and Luís García Valera was a great-grandson-in-law.

Of course after Ella had given me all the information she could remember, I went to the library. Most of my dates, etc., I got from obituaries, because although most of the Drovers lived away from the border country, they still made a noise in the *Banner-Democrat* when they died.

It would pay to study the family chart. I put a lot of work into it. But it was all worth it because the chart was very important in solving the mystery.

The Drover Genealogy

Jacob Drover 1783–1829, m. Susan, ?–1817.

Andrew Drover, 1802–1853, m. Elizabeth Quinby, 1810–1858.

Quinby Drover, Sr., 1848–1917, m. Martha Ridgeway, 1848–1878.

Quinby Drover, Jr., 1870–1916, m. Dora Monahan, 1875–1892.

Dora Drover, 1892–1953, m. Richard Haverty, ?–1932.

EVELYN HAVERTY, 1927–1981, m. LUÍS GARCÍA VALERA.

Benjamin Franklin Drover, 1872–1922, m. Euphemia Bascomb, 1876–1938.

— Jno. Bascomb Drover 1895–? (suicide at Yale).
— Benjamin Franklin Drover, Jr., 1898–1918 (died in France).
— St. Elmo Drover, 1900–1929, m. Elayne Slade (insane).
— Pearl Drover, 1912–1975, m. Cornelius VanDyne, ?–1968 (died in car accident).

BETTYE VANDYNE, 1950–.

Martha Drover, 1874–1959, m. Baker Comming

— Ruth Comming, 1892–1975 (unmarried).
— Allen Comming, 1897–1975, m. 1 Julia Benedict (no children);
                         m. 2 Dorothy Chancelor, 1920–1960.

ALLEN COMMING, Jr. 1940–, m. Marti Johnson.

Abner Ridgeway Drover, 1880–1940, m. Grace Dinmont, 1882–1932.

Dinmont Drover (Denny), 1904–1936 (drowned in a swimming pool on Long Island).

Sarah Drover, 1905–1960 (died of cancer), m. John H. Greene, 1904–1972.

DOROTHY GREENE, 1925–, m. KENNETH RAEBON, 1920–.

e Drover, 1874–1953, m. Horace Ainesworth

Antoinette Ainesworth, 1900–1950, m. Yardley.

Richard Yardley, 1924–1950, m. Eva Duncan.

DUNCAN YARDLEY, 1949–, m. 1, Joni Maxwell;
m. 2, Delou Golden.

Sarah Yardley, 1925–1963, m. DR. ANTHONY HANCOCK, 1920–.

WE LOOK FOR
THE RIGHT DROVER

Helen Delaporte

While Elizabeth Wheeler was taking care of her sister-in-law in Bluefield and working up the Drover genealogy by means of an interview with Mrs. Fisk and no telling how many hours in the library, life went on for the Old Orchard Fort Chapter, NSDAR; that is to say, we had our regular March meeting.

Elizabeth Wheeler's report on the Adoniram Philipson project was read by Martha Doans as though the entire chapter had not been fully informed on all developments through the *Banner-Democrat*, Station WXZ–TV, and the United Telephone System. But the ladies enjoyed hearing about it all over again, and there was general sensation, which of course was to be expected and which accounted for the large attendance. The daughters agreed that now that the grave had been located and Adoniram had been fully authenticated, and the marker, ordered in February, had arrived, we should proceed as soon as possible in placing it and holding the ceremony. The weather was now promising to be pleasant, and Margaret

Chalmers said that she thought she could get a man to mix the cement into which we have to set the bronze marker. Consequently it was moved, seconded, discussed, and passed that the appropriate ceremony should be held on April 6, just two weeks before our April meeting.

Personally, since I had got the Holy Week services out of the way, the ladies could have scheduled anything on any day in April and it would have been all right with me.

When Elizabeth brought me her beautifully detailed genealogy of the Drover family on the Tuesday after our meeting, I sat down and studied it very carefully. Quite apart from its connection with our mystery, I was fascinated by what it said about human history. The Drovers—that is, the ones that do not come down from Quinby Drover—are widely scattered through the hollows and coves of our mountains. And they are reported not infrequently in our papers for murder, theft, moonshining, and sundry other peccadillos.

Considering that Quin's brood died of suicide, drowning, a car accident, and enemy action, the family of old Quin Drover, like their cousins, experienced more violence than we like to admit is normal for the general run of Americans. Most of them died rather young.

All told, the main difference between the respectable Drovers and the disreputable cousins was money. And I wondered if perhaps money had not kept some of Quin's own clan out of jail.

Interesting as I found the genealogy of the Drover family, it was of value in solving the mystery only because it gave us some names—probably the only names we would have—of people in our area in whom Luís García was likely to have had any interest. And though García might have come to Borderville to see somebody else, it was highly unlikely—in fact unquestionably so. One thing proved this; the fact that neither Allen Comming nor Duncan Yardley nor Anthony Hancock nor Dorothy Green nor Bettye VanDyne had come forward when the corpse was identified. Thus Elizabeth's chart furnished us with a perfect list of suspects.

On the face of it, I was prepared to see complicity in the whole family. But I realized that only one could have struck the blow that killed.

A cast of characters to be thoroughly investigated! I told myself. And I was going to investigate quite thoroughly.

When Henry came home, I had him sit down immediately and look at Elizabeth's work.

He was impressed and said he would be sure to put Elizabeth on his payroll next time he had an involved estate to settle.

"Now this first Quinby Drover—" Henry observed, "I believe his will was not probated in Virginia."

Elizabeth had already told me about that. "He was living in Collinwood, New Jersey, when he died," I said.

"Yes," Henry replied. "However, the estate is a legal curiosity of interest in the Commonwealth of Virginia."

"How so?"

"I understand that each of the descendants received an undivided interest. That happens sometimes, although in this case the repercussions continued for an unusually long period and generated quite a bit of legal business from time to time. Let's see. Nineteen seventeen to nineteen eighty-nine—that is seventy-two years. The mischievous effects of that will have probably been felt by each of these people Miss Elizabeth has so neatly listed here."

"But, Henry, how complicated that must be!"

"Well, no, not necessarily. Do you recall a slot in the ten forty form that calls for income from an estate? That slot was made for just such people as the Drovers. For that matter, you and your brother get some money from your mother's estate and there have been no legal problems yet. But if you wanted to sell your mother's apartment house in Harrisburg and Bert, let's say, didn't want to sell, there could be some real unpleasantness and perhaps a series of lawsuits. Usually joint ownership becomes either burdensome or unprofitable and an agreement is reached so that the property can be managed in an economical manner."

"How much do you suppose could be involved in this undivided estate?"

"I don't know," Henry said, "I never heard that Allen Comming did a great deal of business. If there is no more than that transfer business, he would probably have to divide the profit with the living heirs. But of course there is likely to be other capital invested that we don't know about—possibly land or coal leases. But I would think that had been mined out long ago.

"If you want to find out about the Drover wealth, I'd say the best person to ask would be Angus Redloch."

"Is that old man still alive?" I asked. I remembered that when we first moved to Borderville, Mr. Redloch was generally conceded to be a museum piece—an attorney who had "read law" and practiced in a dingy little office over a store on Crowder Street.

"I think he says he is ninety-nine years old."

"In a rest home, I suppose."

"Not at all. He still goes to his office every day. And he handles the business of two or three old ladies. Once in a great while I see him in the courthouse."

There is something about our mountains that makes people live and live and live—at least some people.

The very next day I made up my mind to see Mr. Redloch. I conceived of him as so fragile that he might die at any minute and take his knowledge with him.

Crowder Street is one of the narrow cross streets down town on the Virginia side. It is lined with old, two-story brick buildings, many of them with tatty zinc cornices. Office-supply stores, offset printing places, and newsstands tend to occupy the lower floors, while one or two of the buildings are vacant. Between any two shops, expect to find a wooden door repainted so many times that its surface is lumpy with coats of pigment applied as early as the last century.

Mr. Redloch was not listed in the phone book, but I remembered pretty well where his office was and found it easily enough by the gold letters ANGUS REDLOCH, ATTY. AT LAW still gleaming through the grime of an upstairs window.

Inside the street door, a rickety stair led steeply to the upper level. Every step announced my approach with varied creaks and groans. The pine floor was bare. Frosted glass in the door at the end of a narrow hall boasted letters that echoed the proclamation I had seen in the window: ANGUS REDLOCH, ATTY. AT LAW—this time in black.

I knocked, heard a swivel chair give up its burden, and saw through the frosted glass the shadow of Mr. Redloch as he approached. The door opened and there was the man himself.

He is an elf—a very old one—but an elf. Pale gray eyes, pink skin, totally bald, he has just the shred of a white moustache. There was also just a stroke of white stubble on his left cheek that his razor had missed.

The elf bowed in a courtly manner and asked me to come in. He tugged at the client's chair enough to indicate that he was placing it in a convenient position and asked me to be seated.

I would like to call Mr. Redloch spry, but that is hardly correct. He reminded me of a marionette—suspended. It would surprise me if he weighs as much in pounds as his age in years.

Mr. Redloch himself was very neat, though I cannot say the same for his office. There were dusty papers everywhere. Cabinets and shelves were piled high with envelopes. To my eft was an inner door, the upper part consisting of frosted glass. His law library, I thought—and no doubt it was in as great disarray as the room in which we sat.

He was saying something about assisting me.

"I am Helen Delaporte," I replied, "I am sure you know my husband, Henry."

"Ah, yes," he said. "We were associated in some legal work back in the early sixties. As I recall, there were three parties in the suit growing out of an accident, and each of the parties chose to employ a different attorney. It could all have been handled much more expeditiously by one lawyer. But, then, people have their whims. Arthur Smith was my client, F. D. Simmons was your husband's client, and Mrs. Sidney Young employed Chuck Benfield. He's dead now."

"You have a very clear memory," I observed.

"Well, ma'am," he said, "the secret of success in the law is details."

Immediately I knew that I had found someone who knew things and that I had made an acquaintance that I would enjoy. Quickly I explained to him what I wanted to know and why I wanted to know it.

"Ah, yes," he said, "the DAR murder case. I read of your discovery in the *Banner-Democrat,* and I admire your courage and cleverness in identifying the corpus delicti. I did not, however, know until this very moment that Mr. García was related to the Drover family. Fancy that!"

He hastened to add, "Although I am certainly at your service and happy to supply you with any reminiscences I may be able to recall from what is to me not a very distant past, I must warn you first. If this is murder—and I do not see how it can be anything else—you would do well to let it alone."

Mr. Redloch gave me a very serious look that would have been perhaps alarming except that I could not get away from my first impression—that I was talking to a wondrously fey spirit that was somehow not quite real. He gave me a little lecture on the dangers of meddling with criminal matters and continued to look at me ominously; but because I maintained my silence, he soon went on.

"Well, I see that the ladies are the same as they have always been and that you will have your own way. But I beg of you that you be careful and confine such information as you discover to yourselves and to the commonwealth attorney. You must not let it be widely known that you are engaged in any sort of inquiry that might endanger those who perpetrated the murder, or you will in all probability find that they will endanger you.

"Now, as to the Drover estate, I do recall off hand a number of things that may be of interest or even of some profit to you. My late partner, Colonel Harvey Boyd, under whom I read law and with whom I began my practice, handled quite a number of matters for old Quinby Drover himself. This would be back in the nineties—possibly the eighties—long, of course, before my time.

"You see, I came into the office when I was seventeen years old. That was in nineteen ten. I remained in the office reading law until I was old enough to take the bar examination. Then I was admitted to the firm as a junior partner. Then when I was mustered out in nineteen nineteen, Colonel Boyd as a patriotic gesture made me a full partner. (He, of course has served in the war of sixty-one.)

"I first saw Quinby Drover about nineteen eleven or nineteen twelve. He had mined some coal property, for which he had not secured a proper lease. The land, it turned out, was not in fact the property of the individuals with whom he had exercised an agreement; and the actual owners sued him for three-quarters of a million dollars. It was fought up to the supreme court in Richmond, where old Quin lost his case.

"I have heard the rumor that Quin had spent over one

hundred thousand dollars on high-powered lawyers from New York as well as some of Virginia's most brilliant attorneys.

"We were employed in a minor way on the other side. But the thing that is interesting is that when the verdict was handed down, within five minutes' time, Quin discharged the judgment with a check for the full amount drawn on the Morgan Bank in New York City.

"Now, in those days that was something! The fact is that I am still impressed."

I murmured some encouraging inanity to fill in a pause. Mr. Redloch seemed momentarily to have escaped into the distant scene.

"Well," he came back briskly to the present, "that will give you some idea of the wealth the Drovers had at one time. But a great deal of it evaporated quite suddenly with the Eighteenth Amendment.

"Oh, yes, Quin's original fortune was made with Dixie Rose Whiskey. It was good stuff too. In making whiskey, the water is as important as the technique, and Quin certainly had both. It would be hard to say whether Quin made more out of his coal or out of his whiskey.

"Be that as may be, the whiskey distillery closed and the business came to an abrupt halt when the Volstead Act was passed. Indeed, indeed!

"It was a great joke, you see. Quin had made the fortune while his moonshining relatives back in the hills worked just as hard at making whiskey but made little money from it. When Prohibition came in, the tables were turned. There was no way by which Quin could continue distilling in a clandestine way, supplying bootleggers and so on. He was too well known, you see."

Once more Mr. Redloch retreated into the past. I opened

my purse and took out the genealogy Elizabeth had made for us.

"I have here," I said, "a genealogical table of the family. Perhaps it will call something to mind that might prove helpful."

Mr. Redloch took the paper, felt around in a drawer, and produced a large reading glass. I noticed for the first time that there was a tremor in his hand.

"Tut, tut, tut," he said as he perused the genealogy.

"Denny Drover! I hadn't thought of him for many a long year.

"He was a very good-looking boy—had golden curls and blue eyes. All the ladies felt maternal toward him.

"Denny's aunt, Mrs. Baker Comming—oh, she was something! Had a place at Big Branch. I suppose you know about Big Branch. It's all under the lake now, and there was a good deal of bad feeling toward TVA for destroying such a desirable area. Big Branch was quite the resort in its day. There were cabins along the branch and near it on the Holston— nice places, summer homes, you understand. There was a trolley from Borderville, and the best families would move out there as soon as school was over and stay until school took up again in September.

"Baker Comming was president of the Borderville National Bank, which was Quin's bank here; and of course they had a lovely place out there with wide porches all around it. There were young people of all ages, so to speak, out there all summer long. It had everything one could expect of Asheville or any of the better-known resorts.

"Well, Denny's mother always came for a month, usually August, with her sister-in-law, who was of course old Quin's daughter. And as Denny grew older, he was quite a buck.

"He got a young lady in a family way when he was about nineteen. When the girl's father expected him to do something about it, Denny took the train back north in a hurry. The girl's parents threatened suit for breach of promise. At that point it developed that there was another young woman in a family way, also courtesy of Denny Drover. The second family—not people of consequence at all—took a great notion to make a big thing of it and sue the Drovers for a great sum. One of the suits was actually filed.

"Abner, Denny's father, was the youngest of old Quin's children. And in that family, the younger the children were, the more pretense of social standing was maintained. It was one of those things that are talked about out of all proportion. I have heard the figure of fifty thousand dollars for both girls. I feel sure that Denny's father settled the matter for less than that—out of court, of course. Nevertheless the two girls are said to have come out of it very well financially. One now lives in Knoxville, and I do not know what happened to the other. Denny was always in scrapes—drank quite a bit. I've no idea how much was spent, all told, on getting him out of trouble."

During this discourse Mr. Redloch had put down his reading glass. Now he picked it up again and waved it over the page trying to find the place where he had seen the name of Denny Drover. At last he found it.

"Now, Abner Drover," he said, taking up his discourse again, "that's Denny's father—he had the worst head for business of any of the three sons, and he was the only one who lived long enough to have an effect on the estate."

Once more the reading glass went down.

"That estate is very interesting—you know the will was probated in New Jersey. There was quite a thing about it too. The Commonwealth of Virginia was very eager to reap a whopping big tax in that matter, and the residency of old Quin was not finally adjudicated until about ten years after Quin died.

"Old Quin was a proud man," Mr. Redloch said with a conspiratorial lowering of his voice. "Yes, he wanted his family to rank with the best, and he did not have very excellent material to work with there. Well, he figured that if he could keep the family industries together—because there was the whiskey, timber, coal, the railroad, and banking, in addition to things like his holdings in such items as AT&T, Pullman, and Waters Pierce—if he could just keep them dependent on those industries and keep the industries going after his death, don't you see, they would all still be dependent on the central empire he had set up—and it would all be a monument to his genius. Somehow he thought it would work.

"The will, as I recall, more or less left a certain sum, say seven hundred fifty thousand dollars, to each of the children, a huge sum then, with each child receiving an undivided interest in the residue, that is, the various businesses—the bulk of the estate—which might have worked if he had set up a trust in such a way that none of the heirs, they being such as they were, could in any way control the businesses."

I said that Henry had explained that the undivided interest would go on as long as all parties were satisfied, but that there would be major trouble if they did not.

"Yes, indeed," Mr. Redloch said. "I am sure that all of Quin's legal advice was against what he did. But some people prefer their own opinions. And indeed there would still be litigation about that estate except for the fact that by the time the third generation became involved, the estate was severely diminished.

"First there went the liquor. Then the mines played out, and without Quin to direct the company, leases that Drover Coal might have expected to secure had a way of going to other people; and then there were so many leases that either lapsed or proved unprofitable. Let's not forget trouble with the unions.

"And there was the crash in nineteen twenty-nine. I have no doubt that the stocks in those wonderful industries like AT&T and so on had been sold to make cash distribution to the individual heirs. In the thirties it was the easiest thing in the world to lose money in any business.

"They lost the railroad, and the banks went under. The transfer business—that was the only thing left. That was a kind of adjunct to the rail line. It's still going—Borderville Transfer it's called now. There are possibly some other properties that make a return, but I doubt if there is much besides what I have mentioned."

I thanked Mr. Redloch and made the proper noises about being pleased to make his acquaintance. He was, however, scanning Elizabeth's genealogical chart through his reading glass again.

"Now here's a thing." he said. "Kenneth Raebon!"

Mr. Redloch went into suspended animation for two or three seconds.

"Yes," I said.

"Kenneth Raebon," he began again. "Of course all that we have been saying is in strictest confidence; but this one is still alive. I have had experience with him—oh, not in connection with the Drover estate. But I assure you that he is a very slippery customer indeed."

Once more there was the suspended animation. When at last Mr. Redloch began again, his voice was conspiratorial. "Kenneth Raebon grew up in Hogg's Gap; and when he got out of law school, he went into practice with Cornfield Simmons. (He was called Cornfield because he was fond of telling the jury that he was a simple boy who learned his law in the cornfield.) By the time Raebon joined the firm, Cornfield was like I am now, mostly retired; but he would tell Kenneth what to do, and Kenneth would do it.

"Well, Simmons and Raebon were somehow involved with the Drover estate—mostly because they were the only legal firm in Hogg's Gap. So one time, old Kenneth went up to New Jersey on estate business and saw Sarah Drover's only girl, Dorothy. Kenneth Raebon didn't need Cornfield to tell him what to do in a case like that.

"They tell me that Dorothy is none too bright; but that didn't stop Raebon from marrying her and getting himself made principal attorney for the estate. I imagine he has been drawing a good income from handling and mishandling what's left of the estate, but don't ever tell anybody I said it."

"Mr. Redloch," I said, "do you suppose there could still be enough of the Drover money left to be the cause of Luís García's murder?"

A curious little chuckle rattled about in the old gentleman's weasand. "Money," he said, "or the lack of it, my dear young lady, is the cause of most things."

The root of all evil! Certainly if the criminal lacks it and the victim has it. But I didn't see how anyone would profit by the death of a concert artist.

"I have no idea how much Drover money is left. But I am sure your husband will bear me out that we are often surprised to find a source of money in an estate after we have supposed the till has long been empty."

I thanked Mr. Redloch again for his time and kindness.

"As the remainder of my life becomes shorter and shorter," he said as he got up from his chair, "I find that fewer and fewer people want my time."

He saw me to the door and bowed me out.

I went right home and jotted down notes on all that Mr. Redloch had said. Then I combed my notes carefully to see if there was anything of value in them.

I had a far better picture of the Drover family and the wealth old Quin had heaped up. And I knew also that the wealth was for the most part gone. Old Quin was undoubtedly a rascal, who seemed to furnish the moral lesson that the success of this world is fleeting. How my grandmother would have gloried in such an outcome!

I studied the genealogical chart again. Martha and Jane could not be expected in their day to manage involved properties because they were mere women. On the other hand, neither Martha nor Jane seemed to have excelled in the things that wealthy women of that generation were expected to do. Franklin, whose children had a talent for coming to unfortunate ends, seems not to have had it in him to take hold of the family affairs. And the offspring of Abner could hardly have been expected to handle responsibility. As for young Quinby—well, he died before his father. It really looked as though Allen Comming and the Borderville Transfer were the core of whatever Drover estate might remain.

Of course, I knew where the place was—on the Tennessee side across the freeway from the bluff. It was a group of buildings at the foot of a steep slope. And then I seemed to remember something on top of the hill. It was kept painted and in good repair, but as to the amount of business that went on there, I had no notion.

On Elizabeth's chart I ran a line under the living descendants and others who might be considered their heirs. They were:

Allen Comming, Jr.
Duncan Yardley
Dr. Anthony Hancock
Dorothy and Kenneth Raebon
Bettye VanDyne

Of the same generation had been the late Luís García Valera.
The list seemed to represent six shares of the estate if García
was included. Whether the six received equal or unequal
shares from whatever income came from the remaining estate, there wouldn't be much there. And I couldn't believe
that such a division of the profits from Borderville Transfer
would amount to very much.

Just to see how it might work, I tried to imagine how the
business went on. I assumed that the services of the Borderville Transfer were engaged one hundred times a year. I
assumed further that transfer charges averaged $40,000 per
job, though that seemed excessive. Then I estimated salaries
for loaders and drivers, taxes, upkeep on the trucks—just a
guess, of course—but the best I could make of it was that
there might be $60,000 a year from it, and part of that would
have to go to the heirs. Perhaps Allen Comming paid himself
$50,000. Impossible! I knew very well that Allen and Marti
Comming had a life-style that would require more than that.
It couldn't possibly be derived altogether from Borderville
Transfer.

So what were the other Drovers living on? I thought it
would be very interesting to know.

As I was searching my desk a few days ago, I found again
a scrap of paper upon which on that afternoon I had jotted
down the names of each surviving member of the Drover clan
and added such addresses as I could find in the telephone
book.

Allen Comming, Jr.   713 Deer Run,
                            Borderville, VA
Duncan Yardley   131 Turner's Hill Drive,
                            Borderville, TN
Dr. Anthony Hancock   ?

| Dorothy and Kenneth Raebon | Hogg's Gap |
| Bettye VanDyne | Rt. 3, Mason's Forge, TN |

Mason's Forge is a crossroad about four miles from the airport.

After my interesting tête-à-tête with Mr. Redloch, I decided Henry Delaporte could take me out to dinner that evening because I was going to spend the afternoon driving around investigating the scale of living of Allen Comming, Duncan Yardley, and Bettye VanDyne and would not have time to prepare a meal.

I lunched on a sandwich and a gulp of instant and drove out to Deer Run in the Pontiac.

Deer Run is a wandering trail of asphalt that continues Hoffman Boulevard, which is quite an impressive avenue and formerly the best area in which to live on the Tennessee side. Some forty years ago a few venturesome souls moved beyond the corporation limits to build expansive dwellings along a farm road that had just been paved.

We have several friends on Deer Run, but they aren't close friends, and we do not see them very often. Consequently I have a general idea of the houses out there, but I did not recognize the Comming house from its number. Nevertheless the Comming address sounded like money to me, and I intended to secure what Henry calls "eyeball evidence."

It is beautiful out that way. Our famed Appalachian spring was now upon us. The dogwoods were blooming everywhere. Their blossoms floated in the pale sunlight like great clouds of snowflakes that had somehow forgotten how to fall. It made me glad that I had been forced at the Baldwin School to memorize:

> *Blow, trumpets, blow.*
> *The world is white with may.*

Deer Run winds considerably and crosses the "run" itself several times so that one who drives along it sees very little of the road ahead at any one time. Consequently I wasn't really aware that I had arrived at 713 until I was actually there.

I stopped and looked.

"So that's it!" I said.

It was the old Dr. Caswell house. I say "old"—it was built just before the Second World War when the best materials were to be had at little expense. Dr. Caswell and his wife were much beloved and are said to have entertained, not lavishly but graciously. Mrs. Caswell was a widow when we came to Borderville, and I have been in the house a few times.

After Mrs. Caswell died, the house changed hands now and then. The last time I had seen it, it was looking quite run down.

But not now!

It had become an absolutely beautiful house.

The lawn sweeps up from the road with dogwoods here and there toward the sides. A long gravel drive climbs the hill and curves in front of the house to disappear around behind on the left.

The material is tapestry brick in shades of red and brown. The main body of the house runs parallel to the road, but in the middle is a tremendous gable featuring an impressive chimney surmounted by three magnificent chimney pots. There is a stone entry arch over the front door, and to the right of that there is an oriel window of stone. The effect is Tudor—just architecturally correct enough to be right but still a house decidedly of the twentieth century.

"Eyeballing the evidence" was getting to be a very pleasant outing. I next went to investigate Bettye VanDyne's place. Her quarters were on a wholly different scale from those of her cousin. I found that it was a horse farm—neither an extensive nor a well-kept one. Horse fences that had not been painted in many years went here and there, not always in the soberest manner.

Since the road is high along there, I got a good view of the whole layout. Although I do not know much about such things, there seemed to be a barn and all sorts of pens, and the house was small and a bit decayed. There was an old, old sign painted on the barn that said: AT STUD: DONIVAN'S STRAIGHT-AWAY. From the fact that there was a sulky tilted against a fence near the barn, I gathered that Bettye VanDyne was in the business of breeding trotting horses as well, perhaps, as saddle horses.

There were a few very beautiful horses in the pasture. But, then, I am no judge of horses. There was nothing about the place to suggest that Bettye was making a great deal of money from the horse-breeding business.

Well, thought I, Bettye is one of the Drover have-nots.

I turned around and came back through Mason's Forge to State Road 49, which brought me back to town. I crossed over to the Virginia side and took Maple Street to Turner's Hill Drive. Duncan's place was easily found. It is on a rise and can be seen from all parts of Arley Meadows, which itself is quite an affluent development.

Duncan's house is not to my taste, but it is impressive. It very clearly states: This is an expensive house. No two slopes of the roof seem to be at the same pitch. Rough boards, pickled a rather pleasant gray, cover the sides. All the windows are unusual in shape and size. Although the planting was new, it was thoroughly complementary to the house. I would say that he found his landscaper somewhere other than in Borderville.

I was forced to conclude that Duncan was doing quite well by himself.

After I had done my sleuthing at some length, I got home

about five-thirty and practiced on the Kranich and Bach until Henry came home.

We ate at Ted's Greek Restaurant. The back booth at Ted's is about as private as anything in a public place is likely to be. Henry ordered moussaka and I ordered dolmas. We both had the Grecian salad, and Mrs. Micopolis came over and chatted. (In the absence of a Greek church in Borderville, Ted and Mrs. Micopolis attend Saint Luke's.) I am very fond of Ilena, but this time I could hardly wait for her to leave our table so that I could talk with Henry.

I told him everything: Mr. Redloch—what I had thought about the probable income of the Borderville Transfer—what I had seen at the residences of our three local Drover heirs.

Henry listened. One of his great assets is that when he sets his mind to it, he listens well. It is flattering and wins him great favor with his clients, although I have caught him at times when he appeared to be listening while his mind was somewhere else. This time, however, he listened very attentively to my whole story before he began talking.

"You've been busy," he said.

"Yes, I just told you so."

"Hmm—I really should put you on the payroll and get you to do all my investigative work."

He is always saying he is going to put someone on his payroll. Our children have taken the expression up, and it has become the family joke.

"Well, now," he began, "let's take a look at it. Without having read the Quinby Drover will, I gather that the provisions in it pretty well ensured that all descendants would be bound together in their common interest in the coal mines, the railroad line, and whatever else there was as long as these enterprises remained viable. It appears that the transfer company alone of old Quinby's varied enterprises remains. We do not know that all the surviving descendants have an interest in that company, but the fact that García came somewhat out of his way to visit Borderville would lead us to believe that he had a financial interest here that had gone so sour that he had to look into it personally. We may thus explain his visit here as something of a business trip. His death may or may not be related to the business. But we have to wonder what business could have demanded a side trip on the part of a concert artist about to begin a European tour. It is pretty evident also that Duncan Yardley and Allen Comming are living on a very comfortable level, while Bettye VanDyne is on the low end of the economic scale.

"Incidentally, I have learned that the Yardley boy managed a nightclub in Florida before he came back here—which undoubtedly explains the source of some of his wealth. He is said to be about to open a club in town here. That will require considerable capital. So chalk up lots of ready cash for Duncan."

"A nightclub?" I broke in. "Where?"

"On Division Street."

"I guess that would be out on the west end."

"No, on the corner of Seventh," Henry replied.

"You don't mean it!" That would be right in the middle of our little business district. Then I realized where it was. "That's the old bank building," I said. "Why, that's the old Borderville National Bank building. Do you suppose that the building could still belong to the Drovers?"

"Well," Henry said, "perhaps so. I have always understood that the Borderville National Bank was one of the banks that went under at the time of Roosevelt's Bank Holiday. That would mean that all assets of the bank would have been taken to satisfy claims of the depositors. But the bank building itself may not have belonged to the bank. And if it belonged to one of the family independently of the estate, there is no reason why it might not still belong to a Drover. What was the name of the Drover daughter that your friend says used to live here?"

There were so many names on Elizabeth's list that I had to think a moment before I could reply.

"That would be Jane, I guess. She's the one who married the Ainesworth. And that would make her"—I had to count it up on my fingers—"That would make her Duncan Yardley's great-grandmother."

It hadn't occurred to me to ask about the old building, and Angus Redloch had not thought of telling me about it. It was rather a disgrace to Division Street. Just since we have lived here, there has been an insurance office upstairs part of the time and a dress shop downstairs for a few years. Then there was actually an army surplus store, and that was really very tacky. For the last couple of years the building had been vacant with dirty windows on which obscene words had been traced by juvenile fingers.

More's the pity! It is basically a very good-looking building faced with marble at the street level and two floors above of gauged brick. All it needed was a good steam cleaning and it would have been quite handsome. But a nightclub among all that carved oak and the other signs of opulence that used to characterize the decor of self-respecting banks! The club might use a theme of Roman baths. . . .

"Well," I said, "that's very interesting."

Just then the food came—excellent, as always at Ted's. Munching on my dolmas, I realized that Duncan Yardley would stand considerable looking into, and Florida would be a place to look. But I didn't really see how I could do it.

"I should think," I said, "that Yardley and Allen Comming are front-runners for the role of the villain in this piece. They obviously have the money; and if García Valera came to Borderville to complain about the way the money was divided, it would be one of them that he would complain to.

Still, the money obviously comes from somewhere other than the transfer business."

"Oh, you can count on it," Henry agreed.

"The one I feel sorry for is Bettye," I said.

"Perhaps," Henry said. "Horse-breeding may prosper without impressive stables and white fences, though I would say that we would know about it if she were successful.

"If you were a writer of detective stories," he continued, "I would say that the three younger heirs are prime suspects with adjuncts in the older two—that is, if the murder was committed over something having to do with the activities of the whole Drover clan."

"Yes," I said, "if you mean that the youngsters are still kicking and the others aren't. Dr. Hancock is an invalid. I guess he is not kicking any longer."

Henry smiled. "Yes—that would seem to take him out of the picture unless there is something we don't know."

We went home, and I practiced while Henry worked chess problems.

After I went to bed, I kept thinking about what I had learned and what I hadn't learned and wondered where I could find out more. Perhaps if I found out where Dr. Hancock was, there would be a way to approach him. But, again, if I did talk with Dr. Hancock, he would quite likely alert the others that I was snooping.

There must be someone who knew Duncan Yardley in Florida. Kenneth Raebon, in his seventies, was my oldest suspect, and perhaps the craftiest. Both Mr. Redloch and Henry gave him credit for cleverness. Meanwhile, we were about to have our ceremony at the marking of the Philipson grave. Since Margaret Chalmers made all the arrangements for the ceremony and got Mr. Hilliard to pour the concrete for anchoring the marker, it is only right that she should tell what happened there.

THE DEDICATION OF THE PHILIPSON MARKER

Margaret Chalmers

I don't know why Helen Delaporte thinks I should write about the dedication of the marker at the grave of the Revolutionary War soldier Adoniram Philipson in the Brown Spring Cemetery. She could do it so much better than I. But it's a real honor, and I'll do the best I can.

The ceremony took place at 2:30 on Wednesday afternoon, April 20.

All the trouble we had identifying the grave and the excitement about finding it has already been told. After all that, it looked like the actual dedication would be quite a comedown. But with the publicity connected with finding that poor man's body in the cemetery, National just came through in a hurry to authorize us to go ahead with the marker. And since Helen asked me to see to the details, I thought we ought to put ourselves out just a little bit and do the thing right.

First I guess I ought to explain about the marker. These markers are made of sturdy bronze metal and are nice looking with a very attractive design. They have the DAR emblem on them and look very dignified and handsome. But unfortunately that is all the more reason why somebody might come along and steal them. And we can't have that.

So what we do is stick the bottom part of it way down in a good big lot of cement. Well. I don't know anything about cement and neither do any of the other ladies on my committee. So I asked Roger Hilliard if he would do it for us.

Roger was a neighbor when I and my husband used to live out there. He's eighty-five years old now, but he's as straight as an arrow. I guess country air and country food agree with a man. Anyhow, he seemed right pleased to do the work for us, and I'm sure he did it just right.

Then when the paper predicted possible showers, it simply put me into a puzzle what to do. But Carl Finch, an awfully nice mortician in our town, said, why of course he would be happy to put up his tent for us.

We had the drum-and-bugle corps from the Valley Bridge High School. Their mascot is the Patriots, so they were in red, white, and blue with three-cornered hats, which was just perfect for the occasion. And then the Boy Scout troop from my church furnished a color guard. I must say all these young people handled their job just as well as the United States Marine Corps could have done. I asked Mr. Herbert Rodgers, the history teacher at the college, to give the talk. His address was quite an inspiration. I was so glad that those boys and girls could hear him talk about what this country really means.

Mrs. Arthur Holman is our chaplain; so she read the invocation. As Regent, Helen read all her parts from the ritual.

Elizabeth had alerted the reporter and the photographer. They turned in a lovely story to the paper with a group picture of all the ladies present.

And it didn't rain after all. In fact the sun came out just as the ceremony was over and the daughters—there were about thirty—turned around to go back to their cars and could see the sunshine on our beautiful mountains and the sky so blue above them. I just thought: This is our country, and this is our past, and we are the present, and these young people are the future.

But then I must tell about Elizabeth.

Helen had told me what a wonderful thing Elizabeth had done to run down all the descendants of Quinby Drover. So Helen and I and Elizabeth and Harriet stayed behind as the others left.

What we mainly wanted to do was to see if there was anyone buried in the Brown Spring Cemetery that had the same descendant—oh dear, how am I going to say this?

Well, anyhow, the idea was to figure out who in that Drover outfit had some connection to Brown Spring.

"It could be a Bascomb," Elizabeth said.

Well, I couldn't think of a Bascomb that ever lived in the valley.

"She could have married somebody else," Elizabeth went on. "But that would be hard to find. I just wish those old-time people would have put something more than initials on tombstones. And why didn't they put the whole name, first, middle, and last—and any extra information."

"Is that what you are going to have on your tombstone?" Harriet asked.

Elizabeth said, "You bet. It's going to say 'Elizabeth Euphemia Wheeler,' and not a living soul will ever care, because I won't have any descendants."

We had to laugh.

Finally I told Elizabeth that I thought we would have to give up on the Bascombs.

"Well, what about Comming? Allen Comming is one of the people who might have done it."

Honestly I thought I knew every family in the valley, but when Elizabeth began to ask about specific names, my mind just went blank. I couldn't say yea and I couldn't say nay.

"We can let Yardley go," Elizabeth said. Those were New Jersey folks. And that just leaves Greene."

Indeed there were Greenes. I knew where they were buried, and we went over there and read all the tombstones. But Paul Greene went out to the state of Washington and never came back except when his mother died, and none of his sisters ever married. And Ephe Greene's daughter was a missionary to Brazil and married another missionary down there, and we all agreed that that didn't seem to fit in with the Drover family.

We were walking toward the gate to come home when Harriet Bushrow said, "Now, girls, here it is. See what it says here: 'B-A-K-E-R.' Allen Comming's daddy was Baker Comming, as I have reason to remember. Lamar had our money in that bank when Baker went bankrupt. This is what we are looking for."

Then I remembered that my grandmother used to talk about an Ada Baker who married a dentist from Richmond, and it seemed to me that he was a Dr. Comming.

Elizabeth said that was all she needed. She could look up the marriage license, and what with that and the names she had copied down from the tombstones right there, she could probably find a will.

Elizabeth got right to it, and it didn't take her very long. It turned out that Hartley Baker, in our Brown Spring Cemetery, was the father of Ada, and Ada married Matthew Comming, and Baker Comming was their child.

HELEN DELAPORTE'S RECITAL AT SAINT EWALD'S

Helen Delaporte

People wonder why I do so many things. The reason is not difficult to find: I always agree to any proposal if the actual thing I am agreeing to do is at least three months in the future. When Catherine Gerard asked me to play the dedicatory recital for the new Schantz organ at Saint Ewald's in Roanoke, I thought I would have plenty of time to prepare and that it would be good for me to work on some concert literature for a change and get out of the parish rut. Besides it would give me something to report in the alumnae news, small as the item would be—just something to let my classmates who write best-sellers know that I am still here.

I was right about its being good for me, but I was not right about having the time to get ready for the recital. I did, however, combine my service playing and concert numbers as far as I dared.

There is a distinction between service playing and concert work, and I maintain it with what I like to think of as punctilious discrimination. Of course, I know that many organists would think me merely finicky, but it seems to me that if the music in a service takes the congregation's mind away from worship, the service suffers and the music becomes a detriment. So I am very careful what I play as a prelude and try to make it consistent with what the choir sings, with the hymns, and with the character of the Sunday as it is a part of the church year.

But postludes are another matter. Nobody listens to them anyhow. As long as Episcopalians can talk above the sound of the organ, they will not complain. So I worked up a big number each week to use as postlude and to play later for the recital. Nevertheless there are compositions that just can't be used in a church service—the movement with the cuckoo and the nightingale in Handel's *Concerto in F* for example.

And, of course, when I told Catherine I would dedicate her organ, I thought I would just have the Lenten music and the Easter music and that after that I would have two good months in which to get my recital ready. I didn't know then that I would have the García murder on my hands, though why I thought I was obligated to be a detective in that matter I have not been able to decide.

Well, time for the recital came on; and it was just as it was when we used to play hide-and-seek as children—ready or not, there I had to go.

At the last minute I got my concert dress out of the attic and tried it on. When I looked in the mirror, I could not believe what I saw. The dress looked so young, and I—well, frankly I didn't.

That meant that I had to go down to Buttons 'n' Bows and look for a dress. And when nothing there would do, I went to Cooksport, where there was nothing better. I tried Parsons City and even thought of going to Asheville before I went back to Buttons 'n' Bows and bought the first dress I had tried on there. Organists have problems playing in most evening dresses.

Finally on May 8 I loaded my dress, a small suitcase, and myself into the Pontiac and hit I-81 for Roanoke.

Saint Ewald's was a mission church for a long time before a development of rather stylish houses sprang up close to it. Then suddenly the congregation took off, building a new church of modest size but luxurious appointments. It is "Williamsburg" if you will give full credit to the quotation marks, and it is just a little bit overdone.

The organ, however, is a jewel of twelve ranks, which is consistent with the size of the church; and it sounds glorious in its environment.

I stayed, of course, with Catherine, who is a member of the Captain Edward Norwood Chapter, NSDAR, as well as being dean of the AGO/American Guild of Organists. Catherine lives in a beautiful but unpretentious house that has been in her husband's family since 1838. It is called Maplecrest, and Catherine even has a cook who lives on the place. She and her husband and the whole congregation were most cordial. I was a little uneasy about the Duruflé, which really requires a larger instrument, but everything else was lovely.

One of the parishioners owns the *Roanoke Intelligencer,* and the publicity given to the recital was beyond all proportion. Nevertheless it is very flattering when a parish organist is treated like a concert artist.

Well, I played and I got through the concert all right and the reception and party that followed. The Bishop of Southwest Virginia was there and the whole organ guild. The church was packed to such an extent that the organ did not sound quite so grand as it did when the sanctuary was empty. People, after all, absorb a great deal of sound. But I was still pleased with the organ.

When we got back to Maplecrest, Catherine told me that

I had received a telephone call that morning while I was at the church practicing. It was someone who wanted to see me.

She handed me a sheet from her memo pad on which she had written "Dr. Hancock 983-2648."

I looked at it, wondering who Dr. Hancock could be, and started to talk about something else when suddenly it hit me.

"Anthony Hancock! Is that who it is?"

"You know him?" Catherine said. "He didn't seem to think you did."

"Actually I don't," I explained. Then I tried to think back to Elizabeth's chart of the Drovers. If I had only brought it with me! Anthony Hancock was an in-law. "He's related," I said, "to Luís García—the man, you know, whose body was discovered when our chapter was trying to mark Adoniram Philipson's grave."

Catherine's eyes got large and her chin dropped. "You don't mean it!"

"I do mean it," I said. What else can you say to such a question?

"We have known Dr. Hancock for years," she went on, "not well, of course; but related to García! I certainly did not know that." Then in a suitably sympathetic tone she added, "You know, Dr. Hancock is confined to a wheelchair."

I was certainly eager to hear anything related to Anthony Hancock, and Catherine apparently was equally eager to talk. She explained that there had been an automobile accident about twenty years ago and that Dr. Hancock had never walked since. Fortunately he was wealthy enough both from his wife's inheritance and from his practice that he had had no difficulty financially, at least not at first. But latterly, because of inflation and all the other financial woes that have come along, he had made his house over into a rest home–clinic, which he managed, and it seemed to be doing quite well.

Be that as it might, he had asked that I return his call. Since it was then late, I rang him up after breakfast the next morning.

Hancock had a voice like a Metropolitan baritone and asked me in a most engaging way to drop by to see him before I left town.

My curiosity was so stimulated that I could hardly wait to see him. We made an appointment for ten o'clock.

Catherine told me how to get there and even drew a map. Hancock lived in a section of town that was not new, but it was very decently kept up. The Dutch elm disease had been in the neighborhood, and that was unfortunate for the appearance of some of the yards. And here and there it appeared that older homes, dating from about the turn of the century, had been divided into apartments. But there was still an atmosphere of substance about the area.

Nevertheless, 135 Larch Lane was quite a surprise to me. The house, which was in the style that passed for colonial sixty years ago, sits on a huge, deep lot. It is hedged on each side by clipped hemlocks.

The house is quite large with wings on both sides, apparently added some years ago, but reasonably similar to the central structure. I drew up at the front door and was wondering whether I was parking in the wrong place when the front door, which had beveled leaded glass sidelights, opened and a uniformed nurse came out.

"Are you Mrs. Delaporte?"

Yes I was.

"Dr. Hancock is expecting you. The parking lot is in the rear, and it is easiest to come in through the back door."

I followed the drive around the house and found a graveled lot large enough to park eight or ten cars. I got out of the Pontiac and walked toward a door which the nurse was just opening for me.

"Dr. Hancock is in his office," she said, "if you will come this way."

We were walking through a central hall that was large enough to accommodate comfortably a curving stairway and an elevator, which was obviously an addition.

"Dr. Hancock is here to the right," the nurse said as she opened a gorgeously paneled door. "This is Mrs. Delaporte," she announced as she ushered me in.

It was a large white room with a huge window looking out to the rear. There was a fireplace with carved mantel, an oriental rug on the floor, and an oil painting of geese flying across a sunset. There was nothing about the room that would suggest lack of taste, but it was also clear that no expense had been spared.

I saw two wing chairs upholstered in blue leather and a filing cabinet. There was also, along the side facing the fireplace, a sofa upholstered like the chairs. In front of the window stood a large desk of walnut covered with the usual assortment of appointment book, pen tray, desk set, telephone, etc. And behind the desk, in a wheelchair, was Dr. Hancock.

"Mrs. Delaporte," he said, and again I was impressed with that resonant voice, "excuse me for not rising, but I have not been able to do so for more than twenty years now."

I said something vaguely sympathetic and explained that Catherine Gerard had told me about his accident.

"Yes," he said, wheeling himself expertly around the corner of the desk and motioning to one of the wing chairs. "That brief incident on one September afternoon canceled the major part of my practice and entirely changed my life."

After I was seated, he maneuvered his wheelchair to a conversational distance in a position where the light from the window would fall over his shoulder and consequently into my face.

He was a broad-shouldered man, whose age, which of course I knew from Elizabeth's researches, placed him decidedly past middle life. And yet he seemed, for all his being a semi-invalid, to be in the best of health and much younger than his years. His hair was white, and there was a profusion of it that billowed back from his forehead like that of the male movie stars of my girlhood. His gold-rimmed glasses seemed somewhat unstylish; yet they contributed a patrician appearance to his face. His eyes were blue and quite unusual—persistent is the word that comes to mind. His hands were large and his fingers blunt—not the kind of hand one thinks of for a surgeon, but perhaps he had not been a surgeon. The hands were nevertheless well formed, and he wore a large gold signet.

Reaching into the pocket of his jacket, he took out a leather cigarette case.

"Will you have one?"

"No," I said, "I have never smoked; but you go right ahead."

"You are very wise," he replied.

While he was lighting the cigarette, I searched for a bit of conversation and mumbled something about the house, which was certainly of a dimension that could not be ignored.

"Yes," he said as he put away the cigarette case, "this is a ridiculous house. It was built by my late wife's father, who gave it to us when he tired of it. That was in the depths of the depression, and we soon found out why he tired of it. It was too big to sell, and I was just beginning in practice. My income did very little more than pay the taxes in those days. We closed all but the necessary rooms because we could not afford servants and we certainly were not going to give any house parties.

"But the house turned out to be perfect after my accident." He inhaled, producing an interval during which I must have looked perplexed, because after he had tapped his ash into an aluminum can that he had rigged to the arm of his chair, he explained.

"As soon as it was determined that I would never walk again, I realized that I could not continue in general practice. It was also clear that I could not manage for myself and live in quite the same way that I had done before my wife's death. And then, as you can imagine, a wheelchair is a bulky thing to wheel around in an ordinary house.

"Well, this is not an ordinary house. My late father-in-law built for ostentation—and that meant big. The doors are wide, the halls are wide, the rooms are monstrous. (God knows they cost enough to heat and to cool.) Except for the steps, this is the ideal house for wheelchair victims."

Then suddenly wheeling his chair around, he pressed the button on an intercom on his desk.

"Miss Bowen!"

"Yes."

"Could you bring us two cups of coffee here in the office, please?"

He released the button and moved the chair once again to face me. "It's about poor Lu García," he said in a hushed tone that suggested that we might be in the presence of the deceased. "You see, my late wife was a connection of poor Lu." He looked at me quizzically, but I did not move a muscle. Or at least I tried not to.

"My wife," Dr. Hancock continued, "was a granddaughter of Quinby Drover, Sr. She was a cousin, somewhat removed, of Lu's wife, Evelyn. We visited them several times in California. Wonderful fellow, Lu. And Evelyn was a charming girl. When I read of Lu's murder, I was horrified. I just wanted you to know that I am grateful to you for persisting in identifying the body. I can't imagine how you managed to do it."

At this point I was absolutely forced to give an abbreviated account of my call to the West Coast and the exhumation and all that followed. Meanwhile I sensed that Hancock had asked me to come so that he could find out what I knew. Perhaps it was because he had some thoughts on the matter that could help, but then again perhaps he was pumping me to find out what I suspected. Whichever more nearly defined his motive, I determined to tell him nothing that could not be found in the papers.

When I had finished my rather brief story, he said, "You must have wondered why none of the family came forward at the time."

I said nothing, but looked as though I expected an explanation; and the explanation came.

"As a matter of fact, one of our guests was quite ill that week and had to be sent to Charlottesville. I operate a rather select nursing home here; but in my condition, there is only so much that I can do. My patients understand fully that in a case of emergency they will be transferred to a place where they can get absolutely the best."

Again Hancock paused to see if I would say anything. When I did not do so, he added, "The younger members of the family—well, you know how they are. They have no interest in tradition."

Now that is absolutely false. Young people have a very lively interest in tradition and family if it is presented to them in the right way, and I could have mounted a soapbox on that subject any day; but I thought it best to let it go by and nodded with a pitying smile on my face.

"I doubt if the next generation even knows who Lu was," he said.

Again Hancock was looking at me narrowly. I wondered just which members of the next generation he had in mind. They would be Bettye VanDyne, Allen Comming, and Duncan Yardley. And as for the older generation, there was Dorothy Raebon. At least she and her husband, the lawyer, should have known who Luís García Valera was. Could there be *any* of them who didn't know about García? But I did not put my question into words, nor did I let it show on my face.

"Tell me," Hancock continued, "are the authorities getting anywhere in their investigation? Are they getting any leads?"

Before I could decide how to answer, Nurse Bowen knocked at the door and, after she had opened it, brought in a tray and set it down on the coffee table that stood in front of the sofa. She poured the coffee from a silver pot, learned that I preferred it black, and proceeded through the standard ceremony of napkins, etc. The coffee was served in Meissen cups with a crest painted on them. But the crest was an obvious fake.

Nurse Bowen also had squares of shortbread. She served everything very nicely and left the room unobtrusively. I rather thought she might be the kind of woman who would talk to her patients in the first person plural.

"You were going to tell me something about the investigation," Hancock suggested when the door had closed.

Fortunately the serving of the coffee had given me time to decide what I was going to say.

"The commonwealth attorney," I began, "a Mr. Jefferson, is quite a young man, but there is a great deal of competence there. He has not issued any statements, and so of course I do not know just what progress has been made. Certainly there was a thorough investigation at the cemetery when we—that is, when the body was found. I should think you would know as much as I do about that. Have you been in touch with Mr. Jefferson or with Sheriff Gilroy?"

"Oh, no, no!" Hancock quickly assured me. "I would not have anything to offer that would assist him in any way, confined as I am. Good gracious! I don't suppose I have seen poor Lu in thirty years. And since my wife passed away, I have little contact with any of her family. But I am deeply concerned and wanted to know what progress has been made."

It seemed to me that my host had made the point he wished to make and that the party was over. So I finished my coffee, brushed the crumbs of the shortbread from my lap and stood up.

"It's been pleasant chatting with you," I said as I extended my hand, "but I really must get on my way or I won't be at home in time to cook for my husband."

He said something silly about what an accomplishment it must be to play the organ *and* cook and that very few women nowadays cook for their husbands (as though he would know!) and pressed the button on his intercom and summoned Nurse Bowen to see me to the door.

I mulled this episode over from Roanoke to Borderville. Anthony Hancock had not got any information out of me, but I was puzzled that he had thought it necessary to emphasize his disability so much. Surely he could have assumed that I would not expect a cripple to take an active part in the murder of a cousin of his long-dead wife.

One thing was obvious: Hancock had wished to see me in order to explain why the family had not come forward to claim the body of Luís García. "The wicked flee," my mother always said, "where no man pursueth."

HOW HARRIET BUSHROW BEGAN TO TAKE A SPECIAL INTEREST IN THE DAR MURDER MYSTERY

Harriet Bushrow

Hello! I'm Harriet Bushrow, and I'm eighty-six years old. But that doesn't mean that I am dead.

I read what Helen Delaporte said about me in the first chapter of this book, and I admit that it is almost the truth that I am jealous of Lizzie Wheeler—but not quite. She is a bright little thing—reminds me of a little che-che bird, always with something cheerful to say, mostly about her family or cooking; and I don't give a damn about either one of them.

There! I've shocked you. Eighty-six-year-old ladies are not supposed to talk like that. Well, if young ladies can do that nowadays, I don't know why I can't. Besides, I always did.

But Helen is right. I am jealous of all those ribbons and gold bars dripping from Lizzy; but we'll set that to one side. I guess

the only good thing you can say about old age is that you ca
do anything you want to and people have to put up with you

Now to get down to this DAR murder thing: It wa
exciting though not at all nice to be there when the body wa
found. Of course, having just got over flu, I had to stay dow
at the Pennybacker's house when the reporters got there; an
I didn't get my name in the paper the way the others did. An
anyhow, that was good because the people we finally caugh
were not sure for a long time that I was connected with th
investigation. So I was able to be the "undercover" girl.

It would have been nice to be on TV, but then in the en
we all got our pictures in the papers everywhere. Still, I wa
a little put out at the time. When I saw Lizzie on TV tha
evening, she looked so little and old—I thought, well! I'n
glad they don't have me on that thing—because I am mor
than ten years older than Lizzie, and television is not flatterin
to the old. At least I don't think so.

Well, of course I was interested in the case from the ver
beginning, but I kept telling myself: Now, you are eighty-si
years old, and you just let the younger ones do anything the
want to do. Though I will say this—that if Ron Jefferson ha
given me the brush-off the way he did Helen Delaporte,
would have given him a tongue-lashing that he would re
member to his dying day.

But Helen probably took care of him well enough in th
end.

I think Helen has already explained that I like old furnitur
and have a lot of it. I don't like Victorian. I want my piece
to be early. But I do get as late as the Federal style. Some o
the books call it Empire, but that's French. Or they call i
Regency, but that's English—or Biedermeier, but that's Ger
man. I call mine "crotch mahogany."

There was such a craze for that beautiful veneer with al
those marvelous swirls and variations in color back ther

bout 1820 that all the crotches in the forests in Honduras had
been hunted out and shipped to the United States by 1840 or
a little later. And after that, why, of course there was no more
crotch mahogany to be had until the forests could grow some
more crotches.

That took about sixty years, and it wasn't until around
1900 that crotch mahogany veneer came in again. So there is
crotch mahogany in this century. But heavens! the furniture
doesn't look at all the same.

Well, I have a bedroom completely furnished in crotch:
two side chairs with the urn-shaped plats, an armchair in
almost the same design, a butler's desk, a pier glass, a ward-
robe, a marble-topped dresser, two candle stands, and a tester
bed that I am just especially proud of. It belonged to my
great-grandfather Andrews and was in his bedroom at Pleasant Hill. It is in perfect condition, more's the wonder, and not
a chip out of it or a buckle in the veneer.

Every week for the past 140 years someone has gone over
the surface of that bed with an oiled rag, and the wood has a
depth you can see into.

Well, so that's my bed!

This little antique club that I belong to meets in the homes
of the different members, where there are things that the club
has decided to study. The meeting for May was to be at
my house because the ladies were going to study crotch
mahogany.

I just felt I had to make that bed look the best I could. I
oiled it just extra well—got up on a stepladder to go around
the tester and the posts, of course. I'm glad nobody could see
me, because I look like an elephant in my work clothes
anyhow.

When I got down and admired my bed, it just looked so
pretty that I thought: If only I had a pretty quilt to put on it!

Now, I have quilts. I have some that any museum in the

country would like to have. I have a crazy quilt that I usuall
put on that bed. But it's dark and doesn't really show o
either the quilt or the bed.

I'm afraid I commenced to be envious. Pshaw! what do
mean "commenced"? I have always been envious; it's m
besetting sin. How can I help it when Margaret Chalmers ha
a quilt that I've wanted for fifteen years?

It's embroidered on white satin—the most beautifu
work—the tiniest little flowers and wreathes and little bird
Each square is different and each one is absolutely a jewel. I'
sure Margaret could get $5,000 for it in New York.

I've been trying to buy that quilt from her all these year
Of course, I don't have the kind of money it is really worth
And Margaret would sell it to me except that it was in he
family.

Well, I can understand that all right. But I didn't see an
reason why I couldn't borrow it for the club meeting.

So I put on my hat and went over to Margaret's house.

Margaret has some nice things. She's not a collector, bu
her people have lived here for ever and ever, and their furni
ture was good country stuff. Margaret hasn't much sens
about how to put the furniture together in a room; but wit
good country furniture, you can't go wrong. All of it i
individual enough to be interesting, and it harmonizes n
matter how you arrange it.

As soon as I told Margaret what I wanted, she was perfectl
agreeable. She went immediately and got the quilt out of he
blanket chest.

"You know," she said, "I have put it in my will that yo
are to have this when I'm gone."

"What earthly good will that do?" I said. "I'll go lon
before you do. Why don't you give it to me now?"

But that was not at all nice of me; so I said, "You are jus
a darling to let me borrow it," and I gave her a little hug.

Then, of course, she had to ask me to stay a while. And of course I did.

Well, while we were sitting there, I saw this car drive up in front of Margaret's house. And who should get out but Helen Delaporte?

Instead of coming directly to the door, she went around and opened the trunk of her car and took out this great huge thing—I couldn't imagine what on earth it was.

Well, when Margaret let her in, it was a telescope!

It seems Helen got it for one of her boys. All the Delaportes are very intelligent, and I suppose her son is going into science and was exploring the heavens. Anyhow, it had legs on it and this thing you look through on the side.

"What in the world!" I said.

"I just brought something over to amuse Margaret," she said. Then she explained.

Ever since we dedicated that marker out at Brown Spring, she had had this feeling that Allen Comming was the man we ought to keep our eye on.

"Haven't you got a nice glassed-in back porch here?" Helen asked. "And doesn't it wrap around all across the back of the house and hang over the cliff?"

And of course Margaret has that absolutely wonderful back porch. Mr. Chalmers had that all fixed up the summer before he died, and it has really made Margaret's house, I imagine, one of the most comfortable houses in town.

I guess I ought to explain that Margaret lives on Fort Hill, which is where the original fort was built that was really the beginning of Borderville. There couldn't have been a better place for a fort, because there is a right good slope toward the east and the north and the south. But on the west, along the side of the creek there, it is just a drop-off of about thirty feet. Fort Street goes pretty close along this bluff, and Margaret's house is the only property on that side of the street.

So the house has a little bit of a backyard, but when you a
inside the house or on that porch, you feel like you are ju
hanging off into space.

But to get back to what Helen had to say.

She had been thinking about it and she seemed to remem
ber that the Borderville Transfer—that's Allen Commin
company, you know—has its headquarters and warehou
and all that on the hill on the other side of the creek fro
Margaret. And then the freeway—four lanes, two one w
and two the other—goes down next to the creek. Which
about the only thing that isn't so good about Margare
house. But she said she doesn't notice the noise. So that's fin

Anyhow, Helen thought that Margaret's back porch wou
be a dandy place to spy on Allen Comming. (Helen didn't u
the word *spy*, but you know what I mean.)

Now I am going to butt in on the story just a minute to s
my piece. If there is anyone who thinks we were just a bun
of nosy old women to set up an "observation post"—that's
good thing to call it—they don't know what they are thin
ing about. People talk about what is wrong with our goverr
ment and our communities and all that; but if they don't
anything about it, they are just as guilty of tearing down o
country as the people they object to. Our patriot heroes d
something about the things that were wrong at that time; ar
if they hadn't, we'd still be paying a tax on tea. (Come
think of it, I believe we still do, only they call it a sales tax

What Helen wanted was for Margaret to set up that tel
scope on her back porch and train it on Borderville Transf
so as to see just what was going on over there.

I have to admit that I always was a tomboy. I played spy ar
soldier and everything else with my brothers—Indians!
never would be a squaw, always insisted I was a "brave"—
nearly drove my mother to distraction. Anyhow, it was kin
of an exciting thing to think of being a spy—even at the ag

of eighty-six! And on that nice porch it was just the thing for a nosy old woman to do.

But Margaret is not a nosy old woman, and I could see that she was reluctant.

"I wouldn't know what was going on if I saw it," she kept saying. And Helen and I kept saying, "Why, of course you would!"

Finally I said, "Now, Margaret, we're just going to set that thing up on the porch and show you how easy it will be."

So Helen set it up right there close to a nice wicker chair with a cretonne cover on the seat and a little cretonne cushion at the back. And Margaret could sit there and every once in a while she could just lean a little bit to the side and look through the eyepiece in the side of the apparatus and just get a wonderful close-up view.

Margaret was still protesting—she just didn't know if she could do it! But once she looked through that little eyepiece, she began to weaken.

"My goodness!" she said. "I can see everything as close as if it was right outside the window." And it was true, because it must have been a very expensive telescope. But, then, Henry Delaporte is a lawyer and can afford it.

"If anyone should come in and see it, I would just die," Margaret said.

"Throw a sheet over it and tell them it's a hair dryer," I said. She looked with a kind of blank look. I tried again: "Tell them you are bird-watching. Aren't there some little ducks in the creek that you have to keep an eye on?"

She said, "Ducks would never nest that close to a busy street."

"It's a Christmas present for your sister's son," I suggested.

"He's a field geologist in Ecuador," she said.

"Didn't your husband have a nephew in Ambrose Courthouse?"

"Well, yes."

"Does he ever come to see you?"

"He comes every Christmas Eve with a potted poinsettia."

"And has he got a boy?"

"Yes, twelve years old."

"Perfect," I said. "You are keeping the telescope for your nephew who is going to give it to the boy for his birthday."

Well, she had no answer for that, and so the matter was settled, and I said that I would help her watch Borderville Transfer. And of course with the two of us watching like that, we would soon catch on to anything unusual that might be going on over there.

Now that that was taken care of, I collected the quilt, and Helen and I left.

My meeting went off very nicely at 1:30 the next afternoon. The program was good. Alice MacKey—she's not a DAR—had it, and she had done a lot of work on it. The bed just looked marvelous, and although I was pretty well tired out by the time all the members had gone, I felt that the house looked the best it had ever looked.

So the following day—it was a Wednesday—I folded up the quilt and wrapped it with the same tissue paper Margaret had had it in, and put it back in its box, and off I went to take it home.

"Now Margaret," I said, "What have you seen through the telescope?"

"Oh, a lot of things," she said vaguely.

"Now, just exactly what?" I said, trying to pin her down. Well, she said that trucks had come in and trucks had gone out.

I said, "Margaret, you have got to watch that place and take notes. Now, this is what you have got to do. Get me a memo pad." And she did, and I wrote *time* over to the left up at the top, and then *occurrence* over against that. "Now," I said. "look here. You just sit right here and you can knit, or watch the channel, or pet the cat"—she has this great big orange cat; I can't stand cats—"but you must look up now and then and see what goes on over yonder."

"But there are other thing I just have to do," she objected.

She had me there. But I kept after her until finally I said, "I'll help you."

The upshot of that was that I agreed to watch in the mornings because Margaret works in the literacy program. She has this thirty-six-year-old woman she is teaching to read. The woman's husband has left her and three children on welfare. After the woman's children have got off to school, Margaret goes to the public library and gives her a lesson. And I think it is just marvelous of the woman to have lessons. The poor thing will never get work if she can't read. And then she'll be on welfare for the rest of her life, and we'll be paying for it.

So I told Margaret: "Let's get started right away. You watch this afternoon, and I'll be in early tomorrow."

Now, the whole time we kept up that watching, there were long stretches when nothing happened. We didn't just keep our eyes glued to the telescope; but by staying around on the porch, it wasn't hard to keep up pretty well with what was going on over there. I like to work the crossword puzzle in the *Banner-Democrat*. I am just a little afraid that this old brain doesn't work as fast as it used to. That means that I spend more time trying to think of a word than I do writing it down. So you see, I could do that and watch Borderville Transfer too.

And Margaret took my suggestion about knitting and started a beautiful blue afghan for her niece.

It's a little hard to explain the lay of the land that the Borderville Transfer is built on. As I said, there is a very sharp drop-off behind Margaret's house, and beyond that is the creek. Then the land slopes up gradually and we come to Anderson Freeway. That runs along the side of Turkey

Creek. Sixth Street runs into Anderson a little to the right, as you look out from Margaret's porch, and dead ends there. On that corner just south of Sixth it is level place, and that is where the transfer part of the business is.

It is a big flat area with blacktop on it and a garage and some pumps for gasoline or diesel or whatever it is. Usually you would see two or three big vans painted white and green.

Then to the south of that a hill goes up, not as steep as the bluff on Margaret's side of the creek, but it goes up quite a way. Then it levels off a little and goes up into a sure 'nuf hill beyond that.

Well, on that level space half way up the hill there is the storage part of the operation, and a drive that winds up to a parking area big enough to turn a truck around, and that's next to a big warehouse.

I tried to draw a sketch of it, and it looked so awful that I took it to Ida Benfield's husband, and he drew it up very nicely for me. He's an engineer for the city.

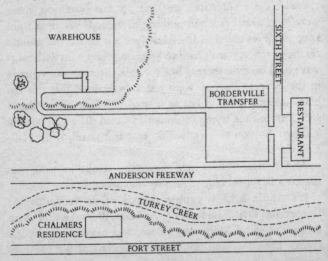

To get back to the main business—

When I got to Margaret's house the first morning and took up my "observation post," I said, "Margaret, did you observe anything yesterday?"

"Not much," she said.

"Well, you must have seen something."

She had it written down. At 3:20 a big transfer truck came in and parked on the bottom lot; and then at 7:35 in the evening a car drove up the hill and went into the warehouse.

"Went into the warehouse?" I said.

"Yes, drove right into it."

I went over to the telescope and took a good look. I hadn't noticed it before, but there was a ramp leading up to the loading dock of the warehouse. (See Mr. Benfield's sketch.)

"Is it still in there?"

"I guess so," Margaret said. "I haven't seen it come out."

"And what about the driver? Surely he didn't stay there all night!"

"I really can't say," Margaret said, "but early this morning, as I was fixing breakfast, I saw a man walk down the hill and go into the restaurant and I *think* it was the driver of the car.

I forgot to say that there is a little restaurant on the corner of Sixth and Anderson across from the entrance to Borderville Transfer.

"And after a while he came out and walked back up the hill," Margaret added. "He went into the warehouse. I guess he's still there."

"That is strange," I said. I was sitting in the chair by the telescope and had my eye to the little eyepiece on the side of the thing. "Do you suppose he spent the night up there?"

"Well, I don't know what else to think," Margaret said.

Just then a dark-colored car—sedan—I don't know what kind. I have no living notion about the make of a car. I couldn't tell an Oldsmobile from a Chrysler, and as for those

Japanese cars and French cars and German cars and heaven knows whatever other kind, well, they are just cars to me. So I don't know what kind of car this was.

But it was a dark sedan. I wrote down "dark sedan" and "8:35 A.M." And when I looked up again, that car wasn't there.

Well, it had to have gone into the warehouse. So that made two cars in the warehouse if the one Margaret saw the night before hadn't left.

Now that seemed strange too.

Then in just a little while, along came another car—blue car, two-tone—and the same thing happened. Three cars in the warehouse!

They were in there—conniving or holding their meeting or whatever for about fifteen minutes—when an old gray car came up the hill into the area in front of the warehouse and started up the ramp.

But whoa! the fellow had to stop and back down. He pulled over to the side—because the black car was coming out of the warehouse.

Meanwhile, the gray car sat there, and I got a good look at the driver. He had on a kind of leather cap; and he needed a haircut, more or less the way the hippies used to, only not quite as bad. He had a great long shaggy mustache. These young fellows with their beards and mustaches always make me think of Confederate veterans. Oh, yes, there were lots of them around when I was growing up.

Just as soon as the black car got down the ramp, out came the blue car. The gray car went up the ramp into the warehouse and stayed for about fifteen minutes.

And then the gray car came down the ramp followed by the car Margaret had seen the evening before, which was a dark green convertible.

Now then, another interesting thing was what happened

when the cars got to the bottom of the hill and turned into Anderson Freeway. Three of the cars went north and the green car went south, which was the direction Margaret saw it come from.

It was just something to think about. It was pretty clear that they were up to something.

To cut this thing short, over a period of more than three weeks we saw the same thing happen five times. The green convertible would come in late, go into the warehouse and stay there all night. We decided somebody must have fixed up an apartment or some kind of sleeping arrangement, because the driver would always come out the next morning and cross Sixth Street to get his breakfast.

Then the same three cars would drive up there, tend to their business—whatever it was—inside the warehouse, and come out again. The route they took when they left Borderville Transfer didn't change.

And I might add that my "Confederate veteran" was nearly always the last to arrive. We figured he must have trouble with traffic—or maybe he was just a late person.

All this time we tried to get license numbers of the cars. But we couldn't because the way the road goes up the hill, we could see only the side of the car. There is one place where the drive turns so that we could have seen the number if it hadn't been for some scraggly little bushes.

Nevertheless we did see one thing about the license on the green convertible. It was white and green, and we decided that it was a Florida license.

It was plain as your nose that the green car brought something up from the south and the other cars met the next morning, divided up whatever they were to deliver, and went off with it.

If you'll look at the map, you'll see that Borderville is kind of at a crossroads. It's because of the way the mountains run.

I-81 comes down from Washington through the Shenandoah Valley to about Pulaski, where it crosses over the mountain into the Holston. All the traffic from up east comes south by us and then goes on west across Tennessee.

So a car leaving Borderville Transfer could go north a few blocks on Anderson Freeway, turn left on Division, and be on I-81 going either way in fifteen minutes. But a car could go northwest too—on 421 through the Cumberland Gap and Kentucky, where it is easy to turn off toward Cincinnati; or it could go on up, still on 421 to Indianapolis, where it would be a simple matter to get to Chicago. It would only take a day to get from here to Chicago or Memphis or Washington or Philadelphia.

Now how about that?

THE JUNE MEETING

Denise Bradberry

The only reason I am included in this story is that I am the recording secretary of the Old Orchard Fort Chapter, DAR, about which the reader has now learned most of the secrets. While I think I keep fairly complete minutes, what I write for official inclusion does not always reflect the entire nature of what goes on. Consequently some of the daughters came to me and insisted that the story would be incomplete without a full account of the June meeting. The minutes are very simple and accurate, but they don't give the flavor of the whole meeting at all. I shall present the minutes first and then tell what really happened.

The Old Orchard Fort Chapter, NSDAR, met on June 7 in the home of Mrs. Donald M. Winebower. Refreshments of white cake with the letters DAR iced on each square, lime punch, and assorted nuts were served from a beautifully decorated table. At the conclusion of a social period, Mrs. Henry Delaporte, Regent, gaveled the meeting to order. The DAR Ritual was led by the Chaplain. The Pledge of Allegiance to the Flag of the United States of America was led by Mrs. Arthur Holman, after which the American Creed was led by Mrs. William D. Carver. Mrs. John R. Carrew led the first stanza of the National Anthem, accompanied by Mrs. Delaporte at the piano.

The National Defense report was given by Mrs. Percy Ledbetter, chairman of the National Defense committee. After a thought-provoking presentation of the relative strengths of American and Russian defenses in Europe, Mrs. Ledbetter pointed out that force of arms, though important, is inadequate without accompanying moral strength.

After Mrs. Ledbetter's report, discussion followed, during which it was suggested that our Chapter could perhaps take steps to support a stronger morality in our own city and it was moved by Mrs. L. C. Hardacre that the matter be further investigated by Mrs. Ledbetter and Mrs. Bushrow.

Mrs. Carl McTeague presented a program on the preservation of documents.

The meeting was adjourned.

Denise Bradberry
Recording Secretary

In order for readers to understand just what was going on at this meeting, they must know something about Mrs. Ledbetter.

Mrs. Percy Ledbetter is a dumpling of a little lady about five feet, two inches tall with thin white hair that has a tendency to yellow. She puts it up on rollers and then combs it down over her ears and back into a bun. She has lots of bosom and wears dark dresses with a small pattern. All of her dresses have white collars with tatted edging.

She has the mildest blue eyes that peer out from gold-framed spectacles with very thick lenses, and her complexion is as white as paper. She has soft, soft skin that appears never to have been struck by the sun and is consequently scarcely wrinkled at all. She wears a little round brooch at her throat. On her left hand is her wedding band, and she wears a gold watch with a black ribbon band on that wrist. On her right wrist she wears a gold bracelet in the shape of a snake with tiny emeralds for eyes.

Where she gets the heavy stockings she always wears, I can't imagine; but her shoes look like the Enna Jetiks my first-grade teacher used to wear.

Mrs. Ledbetter has taught the Loyal Matron's Class at the First Baptist Church longer than anyone can remember; and though she is mild of voice, she is strong of conviction.

It is always a delight when she speaks on any subject, because although the material she deals with frequently comes from the *Reader's Digest* or some other periodical readily found in a dentist's or doctor's office, the seriousness with which Mrs. Ledbetter addresses great problems is worthy of a Supreme Court justice. She absolutely quivers with fervor. And one gets the impression that if Mrs. Ledbetter were to remove her finger only once from the hole in the dike, the whole Atlantic Ocean would seep in and drown the nation.

After Mrs. Ledbetter got through telling the ladies just how many missiles the Russians *still* have and what kind, and how many missiles we have and what kind, she said something like this: "But oh! I regret to say that there is a greater danger at

home. It has been borne in on me that the moral fiber of ou
young people is being destroyed."

There was such awe in her voice that I thought she wa
going to tell us about Demon Rum. But, no, it was a strij
joint on the corner of Division and one of those cross street
There is an old building down there, and it seems that some
body put in a mangy club of some sort. I just supposed tha
it was the run-of-the-mill honky-tonk that we have aroun
here with "strang" band and nasal country singers.

But "strip" had come to Borderville without my knowin
it. The mere presence of strippers would have been enoug
to fire Mrs. Ledbetter's burners, but it seems that this joint ha
a "ladies only" night.

"Actually," Mrs. Ledbetter said in a hushed voice, "ou
young women go into that vile place to ogle the bodies c
unclothed men."

A good number of our membership are in their midseven
ties, and they are dear old things that probably never heard c
a male stripper. They let out one tremendous simultaneou
gasp.

"Yes," she assured the ladies, "here in our own city w
have this dreadful thing." Then, true to form, she demon
strated that she had done her homework. She started with th
Egyptians and marched on through the Greeks and the Ro
mans—I'm sure she got it out of a Sunday-school book—an
demonstrated from history that lascivious carousals alway
presage the destruction of once-great civilizations. I don'
know where the old dear picked up the talent, but she reall
made a very interesting program out of the evils of nude o
near-nude dancing, especially on the part of men.

After about fifteen minutes she turned to Helen Delaport
and said, "Madam Regent, that concludes my report."

As she sat down, ladies were clicking their tongues an
shaking their heads while exchanging scandalized glances

Then suddenly from the back of the room came Harriet Bushrow's decided accents. "Have you ever seen one of these lascivious dances, Opal?"

Oh, dear no, of course she hadn't.

"Then how do you know all this you have been telling us?"

It seemed that Mrs. Ledbetter has a neighbor who has a young woman living in her house who, unaware of the kind of entertainment provided on the nights for "ladies only," had attended this place, called, I believe, the Gold Coast.

Harriet was in her full glory. She was in her summer party dress. It was really quite handsome but perhaps not what one would expect of any octogenarian except Harriet. It looked like shantung—green with white stripes. She had on a white straw picture hat with red poppies on it and of course those famous cut-crystal beads she always wears. Harriet was obviously enjoying the sensation Opal Ledbetter had produced by her lecture. "Don't you think some of us ought to investigate," Harriet said, "so we can make our complaint to somebody?"

Opal was absolutely flabbergasted, and we all held our breath.

"After all, what good does it do if we just deplore it here among ourselves!" Harriet continued. "I think some of us should investigate and lodge a complaint."

Opal was opening and closing her mouth rapidly and looking as if Death had called for her before she could get out of the bathtub.

Then little Mrs. Mursey in her mild voice chirped up with: "You know, Carry Nation actually went into the saloons to fight against liquor."

And Mildred Hardacre said in her very ladylike way, "Madam Regent, I *do* think that someone ought to lodge a complaint—perhaps to the city council."

"That's on the Tennessee side," one of the ladies observed. She lived on the Virginia side and her remark was made in a tone that suggested that nothing so crude could ever happen on the Virginia side of the street.

There was further discussion back and forth before it was finally decided that Mrs. Ledbetter should investigate further with the help of Mrs. Bushrow and report at a subsequent meeting of the chapter.

Helen Delaporte as usual maintained her dignity in spite of all, but I am afraid that I had to look very steadily at my shoe buckles. The meeting closed, and I thought we had heard the last of that matter, and so did Helen—or did she?

I am the youngest member of the chapter. I am a widow. I sell real estate, and I have two children in high school. Sometimes it is difficult to get to the meetings of the chapter, but I have enjoyed the membership of this chapter more than I have enjoyed that of any other organization I have ever belonged to.

Many people make fun of the DAR, and I suppose I do it myself sometimes. It's said to be snobbish. It is not. In fact it is just the opposite. Upon invitation, there is one basic requirement for admission. Members must be descended from an American patriot, male or female, of the Revolutionary War. But once that step is negotiated, there is not a more democratic organization in the country.

In the DAR there are rich and poor, professional and nonprofessional, Catholics, Protestants, and Jews. One of our members is ninety-eight, and I am forty-one. I have profited from knowing these women, and I find it touching that they all love this wonderful country we live in.

I understand from these women, descendants of the Revolutionary patriots, how our forefathers managed to win a war against the tremendous power and wealth of England. Like those staunch old fellows, the Daughters have independent minds; and like their forebears, when they set themselves to it, they carry their plans to a firm conclusion.

So even though I sometimes smile at what goes on in the chapter, it is a smile of pride.

OUR VISIT TO
THE STRIP SHOW

Harriet Bushrow

I don't know what people are going to think of me, but I do have a pretty good reason for almost everything I do.

As I sat there in the meeting listening to the first part of what Opal Ledbetter had to say, I thought I would die of boredom. Opal had a cousin who went to West Point. And so she thinks she is in a better position to understand the military than almost anybody else.

While she was talking, I looked at my nails, and then out the window, and then at my nails again. I thought: Lord, if you are going to take me, why didn't you take me before Opal began?

Then she started talking about this terrible moral menace, and I realized that she was talking about the old Borderville State Bank. It's down on the corner of Division and Seventh streets. It has had something in it—different little businesses and then unoccupied for stretches at a time—longer than most people can remember.

But I can remember, because Lamar had our money in the Borderville State Bank when it went under and we lost our last penny. And then we lost our big lovely home, and there is no telling what we would have done if Lamar hadn't got a job in Washington with the New Deal.

So I have lots of reasons to remember that building.

Well, as I sat there I began to work it out. Baker Comming was the president of that bank and Horace Ainesworth was in it with him.

They were married to the two Drover girls, and so the bank really belonged to the wives. But back in those days, if a girl with money married, she turned over all business matters to the man. And the way those things were managed was sometimes devious—still is, for that matter.

As I was thinking about all of this, it seemed to me that the actual bank building was in Jane's name. (That's Jane Drover that married Ainesworth. They didn't live here, but they used to be in town quite a lot). So though it was her money in the bank and her property that the bank occupied, the property was not owned by the bank.

The Ainesworths—and the Commings too—lost everything they had invested in the bank when it failed; but Jane still had the bank building. A lot of people thought the building should have been sold to make good the loss to the depositors. But nobody was around to buy the property, so it wouldn't have made any difference anyway. It's a wonder the building didn't go for taxes.

Well, I was sitting there thinking about that and wondering if the property was still in Jane's family; and of course that would point to that Yardley boy. And I tried to figure out just what kin he was to Allen Comming, Jr., but I'm not as good at that kind of thing as Lizzy Wheeler is. Then the idea popped into my mind that Duncan Yardley might be the one running that club Opal was talking about.

Of course I had never laid eyes on this Yardley boy, but I knew his grandmother—Tony—and she was about as harum-scarum as I ever came across.

As I told in my "last installment," after watching the Borderville Transfer for a month, I had a bee in my bonnet about that thing, and it struck me that *this* thing might be something like it.

And that was why I began to get at Opal Ledbetter at that chapter meeting, because I knew right then that I would have to see the inside of that club if it killed me to do it. But at the same time, I wanted someone to go with me. Maybe someone to keep me in line! Though as you'll see, I didn't exactly stay in line.

Now, I know that I have the reputation for being bold. The way I behaved when I was a girl was the despair of my poor mother. But there are some things that stump me just a little. Because of what I suspected, I was a little put off with the idea of going through the front doors of that club. Of course, the way Opal was talking about it, it sounded worse than a whorehouse, and I never even dared speak that word until I was in my dotage. Still, that wasn't what bothered me about going there alone.

Well, who was there to go with me?

My first thought was about Helen Delaporte. But she plays the organ at the Episcopal church, and we just couldn't have her going in to look at those naked men. What I needed was a companion like myself, so that people would put our actions down to senility. I thought of different ones, and then that little Mrs. Hardacre solved the problem with her motion.

So it was to be Opal Ledbetter and me. Bless Opal's pure, Baptist soul. It was going to kill her to go into that place, but she saw it as her duty, and I'll hand it to her: She'll do her duty in spite of the devil and Ned Drummond.

I warned her. I said, "Now Opal, you just sit there. I'll do the 'vestigatin'."

Well, the place opens at nine o'clock. With the daylight saving it is so light at nine that going into a place like that at that time is a downright public event. But anyhow . . .

I got myself all dressed up for this act. I painted my nails bright red and loaded my face with all the make up I had. I even got an eyebrow pencil. To look at me you would have thought I was the worst old harridan that ever was. And that was just the impression I wanted to give.

As for Opal, she just looked like her own Baptist self. Nothing could ever make her look different.

We went in my car and parked on Poplar Street—quite a distance away, you see.

There was a time when this bank building was used as a dress shop, and the big show window that was installed then is still there. Of course, that wouldn't do for a nightclub. So they had the glass all painted over in black and here and there great huge gold coins painted on it—I guess because it is called the Gold Coast.

Inside, it was very different. To tell the truth, the room wasn't convenient for a nightclub. It's too long and narrow. If they had put the floor show down at one end, the people at the other end wouldn't be able to see; and then there is the problem of what you would do about the doors.

There was the front door, naturally; and then only one door down at the other end that used to lead to the safe-deposit boxes and Baker Comming's office and all that. Well, you can see that a nightclub has to have a kitchen and dressing rooms and rest-rooms. So they had to put all that sort of thing on the other side of that door at the back. But fortunately the back of the building made an *L,* and there was enough space to crowd it all in.

I must say that given the problem they had, the decorator absolutely transformed the place.

All along the west wall, as you go in, the floor has been tiered so that there are three rows of tables elevated enough to give a view of the whole room. Then there is a long dance floor along the opposite wall. At the far end of the dance floor is the bar, and near the bar an electric organ thing. And then there is a combo that sits there by the organist. The cash register and all of that is actually in what used to be the show window when the building was a dress shop.

It all looks very snappy. The dance floor looks like it covered with some kind of vinyl or polished linoleum with gold-looking coins for a design. Then the tiers for the tables are covered with shag carpeting in shades of orange. Hanging from the high ceiling they have some very fancy fixtures. It almost seemed like they were trying to make the place look respectable. Maybe taking off your clothes is respectable now, I wouldn't know.

Opal and I got a table near the rear door because I intended to give the whole club a good inspection before I left. Opal needn't have worried very much about being seen, for the lights were turned way low.

When we got there, there weren't an awful lot of women yet. So a waiter—they have young men for the ladies' night I suppose—came up to take our order. Opal said she would like a Coca-Cola, and I took a screwdriver. The organist—that was a young man too; just the whole show was men—started some of that beeping and booping that they call music. It was plenty loud enough to suit me at the beginning, but it got louder as the evening went on. Finally the room was tolerably full and the combo came out and a master of ceremonies.

He was in tails and a top hat and said a number of things of a suggestive nature. I was pleased to see that most of them

went over Opal's head, and I really didn't understand some of
t myself, though I laughed as if I did.

All this time the air was getting thicker with smoke, and
ure enough I thought I smelled a kind of sweet smell like
hey say pot makes. I had my eye peeled to catch any transac-
ion if I could, but the lights were too dim.

You never saw such a gaggle of women in your life. I was
glad to see that there weren't many real young girls. Most of
he women looked to be in their thirties. But there were
women there in their forties and more.

Pretty soon the emcee announced the name of the first
stripper. He must have been popular, because the women
went wild, whistling and screaming and banging on the tables.

The lights went down to almost nothing, and a big spot
was thrown on the back entrance, and here he came, a good-
looking young man in a glittery tuxedo that seemed to be
carrying out the "gold coast" theme.

The young man began to dance, and presently he gave a
big kick, let out a yell, and took off his coat. He tossed it into
the air and the emcee caught it, and the young man went
right on jigging. Then in a minute he took off his bow tie
and flung it into the air. The emcee dashed out again and
caught it.

Each time the young man gave an extra big kick and yelled,
it was a sign he was going to take off something else. The
women just went wild.

Off came the shirt. Well, there was an undershirt under-
neath that. Then the undershirt came off, and I'll have to
admit that that young man was right well developed.

The next time something had to come off, he came down
to the lowest tier of tables, swung his foot up on one of them,
reared back and snapped his fingers, yelling while one of those

silly women there unlaced his shoe. Then he took the sho
and tossed it to the emcee.

After he got off his shoes and socks, he took off his trouser
and there he was in boxer shorts like the ones Lamar used t
wear, only they weren't so baggy as Lamar's.

I'll have to admit that that boy looked very sexy gyratin
around in those shorts; but if there is any art in it, it is an a
I am not accustomed to.

Finally he unfastened the boxer shorts one button at a tim
and did a kind of shimmy as they fell to the floor leaving hi
in just a gold G-string a little bigger than three postage stamp

Those crazy women were in a regular pandemonium
shouting and applauding and whistling. And the more eager!
they responded, the more vulgar the dance got.

There didn't seem to be a hair on his body; and by tha
time, he had worked up quite a sweat and simply glistened
Meanwhile, from somewhere they had begun to manipulat
colored lights so that they flashed on him, and he writhe
around there in those changing lights. When he turned hi
back, there was so little of the G-string back there that i
looked like he was totally nude. I didn't dare look at Opa
though I would have given a pretty penny for a snapshot c
her face just then.

About that time I began to see what the purpose of th
whole procedure was. The young man danced up among th
tables and came wiggling around among the shriekin
women as they stuffed bills into the band that held up hi
G-string. I saw one woman tuck in a twenty dollar bill, an
she looked like she was old enough to be a grandmother
Well, everybody to her own notion!

After he had enticed as much money out of the crowd a
he thought he could, he gave a huge leap, gathered up all hi
clothes from the emcee and went running out the rear doo

yelling like an Apache Indian. The women were beside themselves.

Then it calmed down and the combo quit for a breather.

I whispered to Opal and told her to stay right where she was, because I was going on my tour of inspection.

Taking my pocketbook, I slipped through the rear door. Just beyond it, I found that I was standing in a hall that led off to my left to an office of some kind and to my right to a door that opened on Seventh Street. Directly ahead of me was a stairway going down to the basement. From odors that wafted upstairs, I could tell that they had had to put the kitchen down there, which wouldn't be at all convenient. And sure enough, just about that time, I had to get out of the way of a waiter with a big tray. Later on, I found out that the dressing room for the dancers was down there too.

Down the hall a little way to the right was the ladies' rest room, which was where I wanted to go first. It was done up in fancy wallpaper that didn't disguise the fact that the place was none too clean. I cased the joint and saw that it would suit my purposes just fine. I was ready to operate.

I went back into the hall and turned toward the end where I had seen the office. The hall itself was not very brightly lighted, which was all to the good for my purposes. I boldly opened the office door and walked quickly into the room.

There were two men sitting there on either side of a big desk. I opened my eyes very wide.

"Oh, I am *so* sorry," I said. "I thought this was the ladies' room."

Now, who on earth could make such a dumb mistake? An old woman eighty-six years old can. That's who. And she can get away with more than that too.

I told the men I was eighty-six years old; and while I was saying it, I kept coming into the room.

"I asked them out there," I said in a dazed kind of voice "and they said the ladies' room was to the left."

One of the men had got his cigar out of his mouth and wa about to tell me to go about my business, but I was not read to let him tell me to do anything. I just came on up to the desl and rested my hand on it with my pocketbook hanging from my wrist. "You know we old ladies get mixed up sometimes and you just have to put up with us."

Then I made a motion as if I was going to lift my hand fo something and let the pocketbook upset a stack of magazine on the corner of the desk. Some of them slid off onto th floor.

"Oh, my goodness," I said in the most authentic confusion you ever saw. "Look what I have done!" and I began to reach down to pick up the magazines. Of course, the young mar behind the desk got up immediately. "I'll get those things. I' get those things," he said.

"No, no," I said, and I replaced one of the magazines or the desk. He picked up the rest. The two of them fussed around arranging them in a stack. By that time they certainly were disgusted. I said to the one who had been seated at the desk, "Are you the manager of this club?"

The other man said, "Jesus Christ!" in sort of an under- tone.

I turned and got my first good look at him. And would you believe it? He was one of those drivers we had seen at Border- ville Transfer—the dark one that always reminds me of a Confederate veteran. He looked different because he had or a suit.

"Clear out, Joe. I'll take care of this, and we can do the other stuff later," the younger man said.

Then he looked at me and said, "I am the owner."

"And what is your name?" I asked.

"Dunk Yardley," he answered.

So you see I had him.

"Oh," I said, "you aren't Tony Yardley's boy are you?"

"Grandson," he muttered.

"Of course! Of course!" I beamed. "I used to know Tony so well—I guess it was sixty years ago. She was one great old gal. We used to cut up together.

"Well, Dunk, you certainly have a fine club here. How long have you been open for business?"

He said he had opened in the last part of April.

"Well," I said, "I've been out of town, and I just didn't know about it. Now, if you'll tell me where the ladies' room is, I won't bother you anymore."

And I'll have you know that he personally escorted me to the ladies' room! I went in, and he probably thought that was the end of the episode.

Just as soon as the door closed, I put my pocketbook in the farthest corner. I wadded up some paper towels and put them over it. That rest room was just filthy enough that nobody would think there was a purse under that mess. Then I flushed the toilet in case Dunk happened to be close enough to hear.

I stepped down the hall, poked my head into the office, and said, "Dunk, I hate to bother you again, but I think I must have left my pocketbook in here."

Well, that gave rise to a grand search, which was just what I wanted. While he was looking for the bag, I was getting a good look at everything he had in the room. But there was nothing out in the open that would support my suspicions.

I said, "I believe I may have left my purse in the ladies' room after all." And, of course, that was the truth.

So I toddled down the hall again to the ladies' room to retrieve my pocketbook. If Dunk thought he was shut of me, he wasn't; for I went right back to his office and flounced in saying, "I found it! I found it!" in a jubilation that should have won me an Academy Award.

"Oh, Dunk, I'm so relieved," I said as I perched myself o
his desk, accidentally hiking my skirt up so I could display m
knobby old leg.

There is nothing that puts a man off more than clos
proximity to a woman that he fundamentally does not wan
Age has absolutely nothing to do with this principle, but
sure does diminish the desirability of the woman.

So I sat there and casually opened my bag and began t
powder my nose. Oh, he might have felt differently about m
if I had been sixty years younger.

"Dunk," I said as I was looking at myself in the mirror c
my compact, "I couldn't help noticing that a lot of the gir
in there in the club were smoking pot. Are you a dealer?"

He was quick to deny it. He said he couldn't keep h
customers from bringing it into the club, but he certainl
hoped I wouldn't get the idea that he was a pusher.

"Oh, Dunk," I said, "I was hoping I could buy a joint—
think that's what they call it now—from you. When Ton
and I were young, we used to call them reefers." And I mad
up one or two escapades about Tony and what a wild cre
we used to be.

"Dunk, I want to smoke a reefer again. Won't you sell m
just one?"

"I'm not a pusher," he said for the third time, "but I'll giv
you one of my own if you will smoke it right here."

"Dunk, you are a darling," I said; and I'll probably go t
hell for saying it, for he certainly was no darling. He reache
in his pocket and took out a little leather case, from which h
took this little rolled-up thing.

I put the little cigarette in my mouth. "Light it for me,"
said and leaned forward.

He got out his cigarette lighter and held the flame up fo
me.

"Well, I'll be damned," he said when he saw I was i

usiness. "Tell you what I'll do. I'll give you a little present."

With that he turned toward his grandfather's wall safe, vhich was closed but not locked. He pulled it open and took alf a dozen marijuana cigarettes out of a big box.

Now, all of that was going on behind my back because of ne the way I was sitting. But I had my vanity in my hand and ould get a pretty good look into the safe. I could see lots of ttle transparent packages, and I can tell you it wasn't all pot. n fact, if I had been dumb enough, I might have said some f it was sugar. Of course, he shut the door of the safe right way; and when he turned around, you can be sure I was ooking somewhere else.

"How much do you charge?" I asked.

"Just be my guest."

I told him again that he was a darling and threw my arms round him and kissed him so that he was very happy to get id of me when I finally left his office with my pocketbook nd my reefers and of course the first joint that he had given ne, from which I had taken only two real drags.

I went back into the club and announced to Opal: "We an go now."

JOSEPH'S COAT OF A CERTAIN COLOR

Helen Delaporte

On the twelfth of June, Henry and I celebrated our anniversary by going to the Loft Theater in Ambrose Courthous
The play was *A Doll's House*—not at all the sort of play t
commemorate an anniversary—but very well staged.

It was a clear, cool evening with a nearly full moon hig
above the Blue Ridge as we drove the seventeen miles bac
to Borderville. I thanked Henry for a lovely evening. W
don't go out together—just the two of us—as often as w
once did. There are so many things that pull us in opposit
directions: his preparation of briefs at all hours and any num
ber of civic responsibilities, and my music along with so man
other things, not the least of which is the Old Orchard Fo
Chapter. Thank God for anniversaries and an old-fashione
date with my husband.

Out of our silence Henry said, "Are men really as stupid
Torvald?"

"Torvald!" I exclaimed. "He's not the stupid one in th.
play. Nora is the nitwit."

Henry professed to be amazed at my attitude. But it is a fact. If Nora had had any sense at all, she could have made Torvald Helmer into absolutely anything she might have wanted. I have never come across in life or fiction any man so much a lump of dough as Torvald Helmer. All he needed was to be punched down several times and allowed to rise again. Any intelligent woman could have handled him and had an excellent husband in the final product.

By the time we had thrashed that subject fairly soundly, we were swooping down Johnston Street toward Division, where we were stopped by a red light.

One disadvantage of living in a town that straddles a state line is the fact that all streets change their names when they cross the border. For example, in Virginia we were on Johnston, named for the Confederate general Joseph Eggleston Johnston. But the same street continues on the Tennessee side as Polk, named for the eleventh president. Johnston, of course, was a Virginian, and Polk was a Tennessean; and never the twain shall meet—except in Borderville, Virginia-Tennessee.

I explain this because you need to know that on the corner of Polk and Division there is a snooker parlor called Dan's. I am not clear about what snooker is, but it seems to be a masculine activity; and in our area at least, the feminists have not yet liberated it. Which is not to say that women of a sort do not go into Dan's now and then. And if they go in, they also come out, as one was doing when we came to a stop.

I could see her quite clearly. She had a great mass of tangled hair in the style the girls are wearing, and to say that her boobs were big would be the only way to describe accurately the protuberance of her breasts. Now that women can wear skirts of any length, she had opted for almost no length at all. She was such a caricature of what she intended to be that I could hardly take my eyes off her.

But as the light changed and we began to move, I did take my eyes off her and saw behind her a dapper figure—the male version of the same ideal expressed by the young woman.

"Stop, Henry!" Stop!" I said.

Already the car was entering Polk Street.

"Why?"

"Because!"

I was not quick enough. We were already half way down the block.

"Stop! Just stop!"

Henry stopped.

"It was his coat!"

"Whose coat?"

By this time the traffic light had changed again; looking back, I saw a car going east on Division. And in it, I just knew, would be the girl in the skimpy dress and the man in Luís García's green suede coat.

"Oh Henry," I said, "it was—it really was the green suede coat just like the one Jacqueline Rose and that man at Rent Auto saw García wearing."

"How can you be sure?"

"I am sure," I said. How else can anyone be sure except by seeing? "Turn left at Broad and get back to Division as quickly as you can."

Henry did just what I asked. He always does, but unfortunately there has to be a little discussion first.

When we merged into Division Street, there was no sign of anything at all going east.

"Henry," I said, "that really was the coat—*the* coat. Find that coat, and we will learn at least something. But we will never find it now."

Henry had pulled over to the curb. Division Street is quite well illuminated, and I could see the concern on his face.

"If we had only seen the number of his license!" I said.

"I'm sorry—I'm really sorry."

"Of course you are, darling," I said, and touched his cheek with my hand.

"I'll do whatever you say."

"It's too late now."

"Well . . ."

"Yes it is." I kissed him. "Let's just go on home."

"I'll report it. I'll report it to both sheriffs tomorrow."

"Forget it. It wouldn't do any good."

And Henry forgot it, at least for the moment; but I did not. For the next few days the whole experience—from the finding of García's body to the surfacing of García's coat (if it actually was García's coat)—kept coming to mind in bits and fragments. I was assured of the truth of what I knew—but there I had to stop. Henry had asked me how I could be sure, and I had not been able to answer.

Yes, I knew—but perhaps for the present I should put quotation marks around the word.

We "knew" that there was a connection between the Drover clan and Brown Spring Cemetery because there were Baker graves there. We knew—really knew—that Baker Comming's mother had been a Baker. But the two things weren't quite the same. If I looked at it from Gilroy's point of view, I could see that it was a web of supposition such that he would think it the imagining of excitable women devoted to ancestor worship.

And the next item: We "knew" that something illegal was going on at Borderville Transfer because two old women had watched various cars come and go. And yet the very nature of Borderville Transfer required that cars should come and go. Why did we "know" that something illegal was going on there? We "knew" because we "knew" that there was a connection between Brown Spring Cemetery, where García's body was discovered, and the Drover family. As far

as our observations at Borderville Transfer were concerned
was there anything suspicious about cars that drove into a
warehouse and drove out again? Was there any reason why
employees of Borderville Transfer should not garage their cars
in a warehouse?

And then Harriet had reported pot being smoked at Duncan Yardley's nightclub. I wondered if there was such a club
in the nation where pot was not smoked. But Harriet had
seen into Duncan Yardley's safe. That was an eighty-six-year-
old woman's evidence: what she thought she had seen re-
flected in the mirror of a compact with a diameter of two
inches. I knew—or did I "know" that Harriet knew, actually
knew—what she had seen.

And now I had seen a green suede coat and had "known"
that it was the coat worn by Luís García Valera when he had
been seen at the Three City Airport.

How was I to get from "knowing" to knowing? The fact
that I was impatient with the distinction merely kept me from
thinking as clearly as I should have liked.

But then there is the larger question of why we do any of
the things we do. There are easy answers to this question, but
the real answer is sometimes hard to find. I was impelled—
actually impelled—that is all that I can say.

And so I finally went to see Butch Gilroy.

Butch had had to take me seriously recently—not because
of what I was telling him now, but because I had been right
in the past. The identification of García's body by Hornsby
Roadheaver had made it impossible to ignore me. Butch was
not about to get himself into an embarrassment like that again.
He had to listen, and he had to do what I asked.

I was polite, and he was polite, though neither of us was
sincere. I told him about Jacqueline Rose and the agent at
Rentz Auto and how both had noticed the suede coat. I also
pointed out that the color was unusual and doubted that many

of the men in our area would have so expensive a coat of that
color. He volunteered that he himself had never seen such
a coat and promised that he would put the word out to look
for it.

Sunday a week later, when I got home from church, there
was a message on our answering machine to call the Virginia
sheriff's office. When I did, I spoke not with Butch Gilroy but
with one of the deputies. The coat had been found.

Highway 421 is a marvel of highway engineering—a marvel because it is so wretched. It stretches by tortuous route
from Fort Fisher on the North Carolina coast to Michigan
City, Indiana. And when it goes over the mountains, it seems
to have sought out the most dangerous course it could take.
One such patch is to the southeast of Borderville in Tennessee, and another is to the northwest of Borderville in Virginia.

There is a section of that road notorious for the fatalities
that have occurred there. Like all such places, it is known as
Deadman's Curve.

That very morning a car had gone off the road there into
a ravine, killing the driver. And in the trunk of the car had
been a garment bag containing a green suede coat. The car
had a Virginia license, and I don't suppose anyone would
have thought anything about the coat except that sewn into
it was the label of a Santa Barbara clothing store. Would I
please come to the sheriff's office and see if it was the same
one I had reported to Sheriff Gilroy?

All I knew about the coat was what Jacqueline Rose and
the boy at Rentz Auto had told me. But of course I went, and
of course it was the same jacket. While I was inspecting it,
Gilroy came in.

"I guess this solves the murder," he said.

"It does?" I said.

"Well, of course it does. This man had the coat that Valera

man was wearing when he was killed. That ought to be pretty clear."

Gilroy has never understood that the Spanish custom requires that the surname of the father's family precede the surname of the mother's family, but I saw no reason to go into that with him just at present.

I looked at Gilroy steadily for about thirty seconds while he looked at me just as steadily. What his look said was, Don't make any more trouble for me, sister. And what my look said was, You just wait.

What I actually said was, "What is the name of the man who was driving the car in which you found this coat?"

"Highsmith." Gilroy had no objection to telling me that. "Joseph Christopher Highsmith."

I went on home, wrote a few overdue letters, and talked to both of the children on the telephone. About five o'clock I called Margaret Chalmers and asked her if she had been watching the Borderville warehouse that morning.

She had not. "Why? Has something happened?" she asked.

I explained.

Margaret gave a nervous laugh. "Well," she said, "Harriet thought Saturdays and Sundays being the weekend. . ."

"Of course," I said. "When I asked you to watch that place, I never expected you to be so constant. I only supposed that if you noticed something casually, you could train the telescope on it. The reason I called was that if you had seen a car leaving the warehouse this morning, and it turned out that it was the same car that was wrecked, we would have a proved link between this Highsmith and the Drover family." Then I explained about the accident that had killed Highsmith.

"Oh, I do wish we had been watching," Margaret said. "Usually Harriet watches in the morning while I do my errands. Then in the afternoon I take over and she goes home.

And both of us have our Sunday schools. I don't think Harriet is teaching just now, but she is very faithful about her church, and I have the Mary and Martha Bible Class at the little Methodist church out in the valley where I grew up."

One cannot argue about that.

I assured Margaret that no harm was done, though I privately wished the Mary and Marthas in Halifax. On the other hand, neither of the ladies would have been able to describe a contemporary automobile with any accuracy. Would they know a Honda, a Nissan, an Isuzu, an Audi, or for that matter a Thunderbird? Then again, how good would I have been in the same situation?

So I thanked Margaret. What those two ladies had done was far beyond what I had had in mind. But probably it had been pleasant for them.

That call put Highsmith's crash pretty well out of my mind. But it was brought back to me forcefully the next morning when the *Banner-Democrat* headline read:

DAR MYSTERY SOLVED

An automobile fatality at "Deadman's Curve" on Highway 421 early yesterday morning unexpectedly brought the solution to the mysterious death of the internationally noted musician Luís García Valera. The driver of a 1987 Dodge that crashed over the guardrails into Willow Creek had in his possession the coat identified by Mrs. Helen Delaporte as the property of García.

Readers will remember the discovery last February of the body of the murdered musician by a party of members of the Old Orchard Fort Chapter, NSDAR. . . .

Bless Elizabeth and her cookies!

Well, there it was. I had identified the jacket! I wondered how that would sit with Gilroy. It was beginning to be more than a little silly. Nevertheless, we would get our inches, and I feel sure that no chapter in the society has ever taken on a murder as a chapter project.

Henry, you may be sure, did his best to tease me about the news story, and I pretended that I was not teased. But after he left for the office, I was consumed with an uncontrollable desire to go out and see the wreckage.

Although it is a dangerous road, the scenery would be beautiful if the driver dared take her eye off the road. As soon as 421 leaves the city limits on the Virginia side, it begins to climb rather gently. It meanders—that's the only word for it. On either side the knobs rise. Because access is so difficult, houses along the way are built close to the road. Behind them bluegrass meadows often climb halfway up the hills to be met with thick forest growth of pine and tulip poplar. Here and there is a patch of tobacco. In other places the trees grow almost to the road on both sides of the highway. Sometimes mountain streams flash along beside the road. And occasionally one gets a distant glimpse of a peak.

But it is not wise of the driver to look.

The thing that makes Deadman's Curve so dangerous is the fact that it comes abruptly at the end of an unusually long (for 421, that is) stretch of straight road. I am not good at estimating distances, but I should say that perhaps one thousand feet of highway precedes the turn. The road, so straight as it is, does not appear to be sloping downward as severely as it actually is. And one is not apt to realize how fast he is going. So in spite of the sign with the wiggly line and the warning that 15 MPH is safe speed, my heart has always risen to my throat every time I have gone around that sharp turn and looked down an almost sheer cliff at least one hundred feet to Willow Creek.

This time, to be sure, I did not go around the bend, but parked a reasonable distance from it and as far over as the berm of the road would allow.

As I approached the curve, I was impressed by the irony of the peaceful scene. To the left, hiding the curve, the trees rise high and have been taken over by kudzu, that curse of the southern states. Beyond the "jump-off" and not too far away were the trees of the other side of the ravine. And beyond that one can see the mountains along the Clinch.

I walked along the rocky berm toward the infamous curve. I could see that the guardrail had been knocked catawampus.

Then as I stood at the rim of the bluff and looked down, I saw the wreckage. What was left of the car stood on its nose. The lid to the luggage compartment had sprung open and yawned at me like a baby blue jay waiting to be fed.

There is a road along Willow Creek—so far down that it gives one the impression of looking at a topographical model. And as I watched, a wrecker came along to remove the remains of the car.

There was the rattle of a chain. The hook was attached and the mechanism made its sound as the wreck was reeled in with a further crunch of metal on stones. At last it was on the road and on its way somewhere.

It had been a black car—probably nondescript. I went back to my own car and returned home.

Shortly after dinner Henry and I were relaxing in the den when the phone rang. It was Manley from the *Banner-Democrat*.

"Mrs. Delaporte?"

"Yes."

"Are you aware that Larry Highsmith, whom you identified yesterday as having García's coat in his possession, was shot in the head before his car crashed?"

I had not precisely identified Highsmith as having García's coat, but I was so taken by surprise and so interested in the news that I merely answered, "No!"

"The coroner reported it today about four o'clock. A thirty-thirty bullet struck him in the left temple and killed him instantly."

There was a pause. What else could there be? I could think of nothing at all to say.

"Are you still convinced that Highsmith was García's murderer?" Manley asked.

"I am not," I said. "I never was. What gave you that idea?"

"I believe it was the sheriff."

"You asked him if I was satisfied?"

"Yes, and he assured me that you were."

"Well, I am not satisfied."

"Do you have any evidence, other than the fact that Highsmith himself has just been murdered, to indicate that he did not murder García?"

"Mr. Manley, I am not the sheriff," I said.

He laughed. "No, but you would be a better sheriff than he is."

I laughed back. "I think you mean that for faint praise."

"I'll ask you again. Do you have any evidence about this murder? Was it connected with Highsmith's possession of García's jacket?"

"Now, Mr. Manley," I replied, "we know the coat belonged to Luís García because of the Santa Barbara label sewed inside it. The only thing I did was to trace García, find out that he was located in Santa Barbara, and, well, maneuver Gilroy into an admission of his identity."

"And that's all you have to tell me?"

"When and if I know any more, I shall certainly tell you

about it," I said. "Now, tell me something. Did the investigators find any drugs on the body or in the car?"

"Why do you ask me that?"

"Because I want to know."

"Why do you want to know?"

"I have my reasons. Just tell me if they found any drugs."

"It is interesting that you should ask. There was a nice largish package that was at first taken to be cocaine. But it turned out to be washing soda. Now, do you have something to tell me?"

"When I know something, you will be the first to hear it," I said, and that concluded the call.

I went back to the den and told Henry that Highsmith had been killed by a thirty-thirty bullet. He pretended he wasn't surprised, but I know he was.

"Why in the world?" I asked.

Henry laid down his book. "You're why," he said. "You saw that jacket. You reported it to Gilroy. He actually put out a description of the jacket. The word got back to persons unknown, who did Highsmith in."

But wasn't it just a bit excessive? Why couldn't the coat simply be destroyed? And even if I had recognized Highsmith from that mere glimpse of him under the streetlight in front of Dan's Snooker Parlor, wouldn't it have been simpler and more satisfactory from Highsmith's point of view if Highsmith merely vanished in Philadelphia or Pittsburgh, or any other large city?

"Perhaps there are other factors," Henry offered.

Pressed to explain, he thought for a minute and said, "Try this scenario: Suppose that Allen Comming killed García. Highsmith is called in to help him dispose of the body. Afterwards, Comming tells Highsmith to get rid of García's clothes. Five months later, Highsmith, who is something of a peacock, pulls out the suede jacket that he has stashed away and wears it to impress the doll you saw him with last week. You stir up Gilroy. Comming is maybe tired of Highsmith for some other reasons, sees his opportunity to waste his unreliable henchman and pin García's murder on the poor sucker. Gilroy is satisfied, you are satisfied, and that is the end of the episode."

I refused to have any of that.

"Pride goeth before a fall," Henry insisted.

"Save it for the next time you are lay reader," I said.

"Very well, I'll give you another. This time let's say that old Dunk Yardley killed García. Highsmith is one of the strippers at Dunk's little club. Dunk has a wife likely to attract the kind of fellow who wouldn't mind being a male stripper; and a male stripper is probably the kind that could attract Dunk's wife. Dunk has found out about it. If he sends Highsmith away, Mrs. Dunk might go with him. He kills or has Highsmith killed. He rids himself of competition and removes any likelihood of being found out re the García murder. I believe it is called killing two birds with one— could I say bullet?"

I wasn't ready to say it couldn't be. In principle I don't understand why one person wants to kill another person. But Henry was on a roll.

"Here's one that actually makes sense. Let's forget about García. Let's say this Highsmith has been a courier. He has regularly been carrying large amounts of cocaine from here to—let's say Chicago. But on the way he cuts the cocaine with some similar-appearing substance. The big bosses in Florida or Colombia realize that Highsmith has been cheating them out of great stacks of money. 'Waste him,' they say. Goodbye Highsmith."

I agreed that that was more like it.

"Wait," Henry said, "I've got it this time. Duncan or Allen killed García. One or both called on Highsmith to get rid of the body. This time, however, he sees an angle. He can keep the jacket and blackmail the Drover boys. He lets a few months go by. All this time Comming and Yardley, being unaccustomed to murder, are uneasy about certain members of the DAR who are very inquisitive and are furnishing brains to Sheriff Gilroy. Highsmith begins to insinuate that it would be a good thing if the firm cut him, Highsmith, into a more appropriate share of the proceeds. The firm says, 'Get lost.' 'Oh, wait a minute,' says Highsmith. 'I have this jacket. If you don't do right by me, I'll see that it gets to one of those nasty old women in such a way that you will get the rap.' 'You wouldn't,' they say. 'Oh, wouldn't I though.' "

"All right," I said. "You've made your point. There are any number of reasons why the Drover family might wish to get rid of Highsmith. And I really don't know why I care. I don't intend to search for his killer. He's a nobody—probably deserved to get just what came to him. Oh, I don't know why I ever got into all this."

Henry looked at me wisely over his spectacles. "Don't you think you are being a little crass after all the talk about the law and moral fibre?" he said and returned to his book.

The next morning the *Banner-Democrat* had a story at the top of the first page about Highsmith and the coroner's report. The original assumption that death had resulted from the plunge over the edge of the ravine was corrected. And of course the connection between García's murder and the shooting of Highsmith was strongly suggested. Then at the bottom of the page was a story with the headline:

WOMAN DENIES HIGHSMITH KILLED HARPIST

Interviewed by the Banner-Democrat, Mrs. Henry Delaporte, prominent club woman and Regent of the Old Orchard Chapter, NSDAR,

> refused to accept Sheriff Calvin "Butch" Gil-
> roy's conclusion that Joseph Christopher High-
> smith, whose body was found in a wrecked car
> below "Deadman's Curve" on highway 421
> early Sunday morning was the murderer of Luís
> García Valera.
>
> Last February Mrs. Delaporte and a commit-
> tee of ladies from her chapter encountered
> García's badly mangled body . . .

and it went on from there. Manley had made an interview of
our conversation of the evening before; and although he did
not actually say so, his story left the impression that I might
reveal something new about the case. The DAR angle of the
story had just really gotten out of hand. But Elizabeth had
done her thing and she had certainly been successful. I
thought it best to say nothing.

Although the prenuptial behavior of our young people has
changed markedly since my day, there are still plenty of
weddings in June—a fact that makes the early part of summer
vie with Advent and Holy Week for the busiest time of the
year for organists. The church musician is at least in control
of the music of the Christmas and Easter seasons; but when it
comes to weddings, there is the problem of the bride, the
bride's mother, and the bride's girlfriend, who is going to
sing.

It is a blessing that the Episcopal Church has a few set ideas
about music. When all parties understand this, we get on very
well. But there is much conferring, arranging, and sometimes
teaching of the music to the soloist before every wedding.

At the moment I was very busy with the Barnard wedding.
Laura Jean Barnard was being married on the eighteenth.
Janeen, her mother, was Regent of the chapter on the Ten-
nessee side of town a few years ago; and I have known her for

a long time in the music club. Janeen was very careful to include me in all the bridal parties; and since the Barnards are quite well-to-do, my name appeared quite frequently in the society column of the *Banner-Democrat*.

The wedding was in fact a very big show, which Henry could not attend because he was in court that day. So I drove alone out to the country club for the reception. There was a six-tiered cake and a champagne fountain and hors d'oeuvres of every sort as well as an orchestra that played so loudly that nobody could gossip.

After I had taken my share of the goodies and congratulated the bride's mother on how well everything had gone and she had congratulated me on the music and told me that something would be in the mail for me in a few days in spite of the fact that she had given me a pair of brass candlesticks at the rehearsal dinner, I crunched across the gravel to the club parking lot, got into my car, and headed for home.

Driving down Whippoorwill Lane, I was within a block of home when suddenly my windshield exploded. I stopped the car immediately, almost too startled to be afraid. I found that I was not hurt. I also had the impression that a car on the other side of the park had started up and was going away at quite a clip. Not until then did I realize that I had been shot at. I had heard the sound of the gun, but the shattering of the windshield had drawn my mind away from it.

At first I couldn't believe that it had happened. And then a feeling of panic seemed to crawl up the back of my neck. It was horrible. I jumped out of the car and ran as fast as I could. I don't know why I didn't turn my ankle. I did not stop until I tried to open our front door and found that I had left my keys in the ignition of the car.

I fumbled frantically for the key that I keep under the cushion of the glider and was inside the house more quickly than it seemed.

Still in a panic, I called Henry's office. Thank God there had been an adjournment and he was there. I tried to be calm as I told him what had happened, but he had to ask me three times about it. Finally he said, "Stay there until I get there, and don't let anyone into the house unless he is in a police uniform."

I went into the bedroom. I was shaking all over. But when I sat down in Henry's big easy chair, the first thing I noticed was that I had ruined my best pair of shoes.

That simple detail had sedative effect on me, and I had a little laugh, put on another pair of shoes, and then did my face again.

Almost immediately I heard a siren. A city police car came into the drive. The officer was just beginning to question me when Henry drove up. He was followed by a car driven by the chief of police himself. When Henry summons the law, he does a good job of it.

I started my tale three times before I finally got it finished.

"All right, I think that will do for the moment," Chief Carter said. "Let's go down where you left the car."

Henry took me in his Chevrolet. "This is the end of your detective game," he said very firmly. "You are not to make another move in connection with this García business."

It was an order. But at that moment it sounded like a very good order. I was perfectly willing to submit to it.

"And when your newspaper friends get to you about this, don't say a thing about García or Highsmith. In fact don't say anything that they can report in that paper of theirs."

I answered only with a very meek look.

"Now, you heard me," Henry said just to make it final.

He was right. It was the publicity and my name in the paper, purportedly knowing more than I actually knew, that had got me into this scrape.

By the time we got to my Pontiac, there was a mixed group

of neighbors and others gawking at my shattered glass. And sure enough, here came a reporter with a photographer in tow.

"There she is," someone said. "It's that Mrs. Delaporte." The photographer began to click away.

The officers asked me many questions about how fast I was going and how long it took me to stop; whether I had noticed a car on Chestnut Street; whether I had been followed from the club.

I hadn't noticed anything, but one of the neighbors had seen a car with a man in it on the other side of our small neighborhood park. The car had been there since about two-thirty. I realized all too fully that I had been living in a goldfish bowl. He, they—whoever the baddies were—had read about me in connection with the Highsmith shooting and in the stories about the Barnard wedding as well and had waited there in the park until I came by.

The officers found the place where my assailants had been parked. They found a cigarette butt, for all that was worth. People were milling about. Everyone except me seemed to be having a good time. All the while the reporter was taking notes and sketching the lay of the land.

And then the television crew arrived. Remembering what Henry had said, I turned my face away and refused to talk.

But they kept asking their questions, and I kept shaking my head until Henry interposed. "Mrs. Delaporte has had enough of this," he said. "She has just finished playing for a wedding at Saint Luke's, she has been shot at, she has been interrogated by the officers, and you've got your pictures and all the story you are going to get. Shove off."

The media people grumbled but turned and left, and Henry took me home in his car before he returned and drove the Pontiac to the house.

I did not watch the local news on television that night, but

I could not avoid the story in the paper the next morning. My picture was in the center of the page, dressed, of course, as I had been dressed for the reception at the club. I was glad at least that I had repaired my face before that picture was taken. The headline said: SHOT AIMED AT PROMINENT CLUB WOMAN A subhead added: I Cannot Talk About It, She Says.

The story was highly colored and amazingly ingenious as it described the society glitter for a church wedding and a glamorous function at the country club only to be followed by a close brush with death.

One paragraph was headed: There Was No Warning. What followed was a paragraph that said much about my busy concerns as housewife, musician, and civic leader and what was supposedly in my mind as I had been driving down Whippoorwill.

Then the episode of the discovery of García's body was reviewed, and the Old Orchard Fort Chapter, NSDAR, was duly mentioned, and our project of marking graves and my office as Regent and the likelihood that the attack on me resulted from my efforts to elucidate certain aspects of the García case. Inches! All of it inches! I wished I had never heard of inches. This was not at all the kind of publicity the DAR was seeking.

On an inner page there was a picture of me at the organ at Saint Luke's. It had been used several years back when I gave a recital. Beneath the picture was a résumé of my career as a "club woman." It was the most ridiculous thing I have ever seen.

Even before I could read all the hoopla in the *Banner-Democrat*, the telephone began to ring. The vicar was first. He was astounded, but I could tell he was also pleased that it had been mentioned that I performed at his church. Harriet Bushrow called. She had to be told everything about it. I told her that Henry had positively forbidden me to go any further in the matter of García's murder.

"That's just what Lamar would have said to me," she observed. "But Lamar is gone now, and I can do just what I please—the old darling! Was it one of those wretched Drovers that shot at you?"

I don't know why I hadn't thought about it, but both Allen Comming and Duncan Yardley had been at the reception at the club. It was a horrible thought that people who were accepted socially were involved in trying to kill me.

I told Harriet that we had better give up on our search for an answer to the García mystery. I could tell, however, that she was unimpressed by my suggestion.

The story(s) in the *Banner-Democrat* did not end the newspaper coverage of the episode. Far from it. The attempt to murder the Regent of a DAR chapter was not quite the same as a man's biting a dog; but it was near enough to it that the story received more attention elsewhere than any of the preceding accounts of what was now the *famous* DAR murder mystery. A friend in Gainesville, Florida, sent me a clipping from her paper, and the President General (of the DAR) in Washington called me in the greatest solicitude.

I was a wreck.

But it was already Saturday again, and I had to go down to Saint Luke's and practice. With the altar guild busily preparing for the Sunday service and the familiar gloom of the sanctuary and the familiar sound of pipes, reality returned. I was quite content to be just a church organist.

WHAT I SAW IN ROANOKE

Elizabeth Wheeler

Other than looking up the Drover family genealogy and
working with that nice young Mr. Manley on the publicity,
there was just one little thing that I discovered about our
DAR mystery, and I didn't even have enough sense to report
it to Helen or the rest of them until it was almost too late to
be of any use.

It was all because I am pretty good at family history; and if
there is something in a line that doesn't work out just right,
I just go after it and keep on going. And I generally find what
I'm looking for sooner or later. Well, that's the secret of
genealogy: experience and persistence. Because if you ever
find something in a certain way, you remember to look there
again the next time you think you have come to a dead end.
By keeping everlastingly at it, you pick up new ways of doing
things.

Thirty years ago, when I first got to work on my own
family, there were other ladies in my chapter (I was living in

Norton then) that wanted help, and I helped them. And then I moved to Borderville and went into the Old Orchard Fort Chapter, and the ladies wanted me to help there too. After that, I began to help ladies who wanted to join other chapters; and before I knew it, I had an absolute *reputation*.

Well, it is something to have a reputation. And it can mean a little money, because now every so often they ask me to go somewhere—up the valley, or over into Kentucky, or even over into North Carolina—and give a workshop.

I used to do it for $25 and expenses. But now I get $300 and expenses for a three-day workshop. I guess that's inflation. But that isn't at all bad, because there are so many genealogy clubs now; and if they sell tickets to people who aren't members, they can make a little money for their club or chapter or whatever.

Well, the Genealogy Club in Roanoke wanted me to talk about genealogical information in what I call "hidden places" in courthouses. Now, that really does call for experience because the practice of keeping records could vary from county to county in the old days, and sometimes the records never have been put in order.

They wanted me to go up to Roanoke the first week in June. I didn't even know that Helen Delaporte had just played a concert up there, and I don't imagine she knew I was holding a workshop.

Anyhow, the Roanoke club, to cut down on expenses, had me stay in the house of the president of the club, Mrs. Amy Tilbury. That is always the cheapest way, and it is just okay with me because I get a nice quiet room and my hostesses always treat me like the queen of England. And besides, I usually pick up some new recipes when I stay in one of those homes.

The Roanoke meeting went off well. The ladies were all very interested, and there were five *men* in the club. When

you get a *man* interested in family history, you have a rea
genealogist.

Mrs. Tilbury had a lovely room for me—upstairs in a big
old two-story house. There was exposure on two sides, and
one of the windows looked out at the back. If you remember
what the weather was like that week, we had that cool spell
and then it got so warm that I had to loop the curtains back
to try to catch a breeze and bring a little air into the room.

The session on Friday afternoon was over at 4:30, and I was
just back in my room and had gone to loop the curtain back.
I just stayed at the window a bit looking out at Mrs. Tilbury's
flower garden. She had the little dwarf marigolds and agera-
tums, and they were all in bloom and just as pretty as can be.
And then there was a fence and the alley. And beyond that
there was a great big house—just about big enough to be a
country inn. There was a great huge garage, and most of the
backyard was paved like a parking lot.

In the middle of that paved space there was a spanking new
hardtop convertible, white with gray top, and beautiful
white-sidewall tires.

Pretty soon the back door of that big house opened and a
man in a wheelchair came out. He looked like he might be
in his fifties except that his hair was white. There was a young
woman in a nurse's dress walking along pushing this little
chrome wheelchair—the kind that folds up. That nurse just
pushed that wheelchair right up to the driver's side of that
sporty car, opened the car door, pushed the chair up a little
farther, and there the man was in his wheelchair right next to
the driver's seat. Then he reached up and got hold of some
thing next to the roof on the inside of the car and strained up
on it. The nurse pulled the chair back, and the man kind of
moved his hips around and adjusted his position by holding
to the roof in that manner. The nurse came over and picked
up his legs and set them inside the car and closed the door.

Then she pushed the chair around to the back of the car, opened the trunk, closed up the wheelchair, and put it into the trunk. She closed the trunk and gave the key to the man.

You never saw anything that looked easier.

The next thing I knew, he had the engine going and was backing around in his own car! I just thought it was marvelous. It was absolutely fascinating, and I thought: How wonderful that a man with paralyzed limbs can get out and drive around in his own car!

So I asked Mrs. Tilbury at dinner about her neighbor. Yes, she said, her neighbor had been paralyzed for years and it was simply astounding how he got along. She said he was running a nursing home over there and doing very well financially, but it wasn't surprising that he was doing so well with a nursing home because he was a doctor and had had a large practice before he lost the use of his legs.

Then she mentioned his name: Anthony Hancock!

Of course I remembered *that* name! But I didn't let on that I knew anything about him. Mrs. Tilbury said something about Dr. Hancock's wife being dead and how she had had money, and I just sat there as if it was all news to me. But I was thinking all the time—that man has mighty strong arms, and it's only 150 miles from Roanoke to Borderville.

Now could he get in that car, drive down to Borderville, somehow or other get into a fight with Mr. García, and kill him? But, then, I didn't see how that was possible. How could a paralyzed man get into a fight and kill someone? He could shoot somebody, but García was not shot. And then how would he get rid of the body and get it out to the Brown Spring Cemetery?

I didn't see how a man in a wheelchair, even if he was big and strong otherwise, could do what the man who killed Mr. García did. So I just sort of put it out of my mind.

Now, of course I had been keeping up the publicity the

chapter was getting from the very beginning of the DA
murder mystery, and I was keeping track of the number
inches. And it was just surprising how ladies all over th
country were sending our members—and other people i
Borderville too—clippings from their local papers.

So when Helen was shot at by that gunman, the who
thing started up again. Mr. Manley and all the other peop
down at the paper handled it just the way I had showed them
So it was time for me to go into the kitchen and bake up
storm.

Well, the ladies in the chapter were just getting a flood c
letters asking if it was our chapter and all about it. So there wa
quite a lot of interest.

Then I got this call from Harriet Bushrow. She explaine
that Mr. Delaporte wouldn't let Helen do anything mor
about the murder, and now Harriet said that she and Margare
and I had to go on with it.

I'll tell you plainly, I can look up genealogy like anything
but if it ever came to doing the kind of thing Helen an
Harriet do, I'd just be scared to death.

"I can't do it," I said. But Harriet never will take no for a
answer, and she said we ought to meet and put our head
together and—well, there is no denying Harriet.

So we came together at Margaret's house the very nex
morning. Margaret had coffee and a real nice coffee cake fo
us, and we sat around on that lovely porch at the back of he
house. The windows were open, and it was just delightful.

Harriet explained what she and Margaret had been doin
and showed me the record they had made of the things tha
happened over at Borderville Transfer. And it *did* look ver
peculiar and as if something suspicious had been going o
over there.

"Well, I think what we have to do is just go over every-

hing that has happened," Harriet said, "and we'll see if there
s anything we have been overlooking."

So we started with the day we went to the Brown Spring
Cemetery, and Harriet told Margaret to write down notes on
everything we went over.

Then Harriet asked me everything I had run into in tracing
he Drover family, and I went over each one of the Drovers
again and told everything I knew.

After we got it all out there in front of us, Harriet said,
'There is too much money in that family, and they are not
naking it out of the transfer business. That club the Yardley
boy has may be making a little money, but it has been open
only a few months. So all this money he's been spending
around here has to come from somewhere else. Then there
is that lawyer up in Hogg's Gap. Do you know how he's
doing, Lizzie?"

Well, I didn't. But I said that he seemed to be doing all
right. He's the one, you know, who married Sarah Drover;
and they have always been in a comfortable way. I guess he's
still practicing law. I said I would ask my sister in Hogg's Gap.
The Hogg's Gap people usually have a pretty good idea of the
financial condition of everybody up that way.

"That leaves us with Miss VanDyne," Harriet said. "Now
what do we know about her?"

Margaret knew the answer to that. "She raises Tennessee
walking horses," she said.

"But does she make anything out of it?"

Margaret seems to know something about raising horses
because her brother used to raise them. She said, "There is a
lot of expense in it if you try to do it in a big way. Brother
managed a stock farm for a man in McMinn County thirty
years ago. The man had to give it up on account of losing
some of his mares when his barn burned down. There are lots
of things that can go wrong when you breed animals."

"Helen tells me that doctor up in Roanoke has lots o money," Harriet said.

"Oh, yes," I said, and of course I told her what Mrs Tilbury had said about his getting money from his wife an about how he still had patients and kept them in that fanc rest home. And then I mentioned about his being able t drive, because that car that he had looked awfully expensive And that was the first that the others knew that Dr. Hancoc could get out and go anywhere he wanted to.

Then Harriet asked me to describe the car; and when I did she and Margaret looked at each other. It seems they had see a car like that several times go up into that warehouse plac up on the hill across from where Margaret lives. And Harrie said that was probably why they had fixed that ramp, so Dr Hancock's car could drive into the warehouse.

After we had talked and talked about everything, Harrie said, "Now, girls, what it amounts to is that those two boy are living way too high on the hog to be depending on hones money, and we all know there's nothing left of the Drove money. So there's just one thing it can be: *Drugs.*"

It's just so sad to think how that family went down. Ol Mr. Quin Drover always wanted his children to be respect able and all. But when you think of it, he wasn't very hones and honorable when he first got started.

WHAT I SAW AND HOW I GOT THE EVIDENCE

Harriet Bushrow

This is Hattie Bushrow again taking up the story right where Lizzie Wheeler left it after we made our little review of all our facts and fancies. There was no question at all in my mind that one of the Drovers had, as they say, done it. But there was no putting a finger on any one of them.

So when I got home, I called Helen and we had quite a long—"conference," I guess you would call it.

It just seemed that the one who killed García would have to be a man. I'm not one to minimize what a woman can do when she puts her mind to it; but to beat a person's face that way—I just couldn't think why a woman would do it.

As for that poor old thing up in Hogg's Gap—Raebon—pshaw, I bet I could beat him in a fistfight myself. Now, Hancock sounds like he would have the strength in his arms. But García would have to lean over for Hancock to hit him in the face, and García wasn't going to do anything of the sort.

So that left young Duncan and Allen. Well, what about them?

Duncan is the only one I ever talked to—down there at his club, you know. And he let me bamboozle him, for that's what it amounted to. I just don't think he has the stuff in him to do what somebody did to García.

Now, Allen might be different. I picked him out while we were watching Borderville Transfer from Margaret's back porch. He is beefy. He could have done it. But I would think that either Allen or Duncan would use a gun if they wanted to kill someone. Or maybe they would have somebody else do it. I believe people in those illegal "enterprises" have somebody else "rub out" the folks they want to get rid of.

As I thought about it, the person we knew least about was Bettye VanDyne.

That stud farm—was it really a stud farm? Oh, I didn't doubt that she had a business there. But so did Allen Comming over at Borderville Transfer, and that wasn't just moving furniture around. And so did Duncan Yardley have a business, and that wasn't just young men taking their clothes off.

So I decided I would go out there and look at the place.

"Now, Harriet, you're not to go out there," Helen said when I told her.

"I'd like to know why not," I said. Then she went on about how that husband of hers said it was too dangerous for us girls to look into all that. Fiddlesticks!

The place wasn't hard to find, although that narrow road is a regular corkscrew. But after a while I came around the bend and there it was: big sign—paint not very fresh. In fact, nothing looked like it had been painted in a long time.

I pulled over near the gate—as far off the road as I could. I guess I should explain that the road is higher than Miss VanDyne's place. The fence runs right along beside the road, and then there is this gate, and the lane just on the other side of the gate goes down quite a bit.

There was lots of gravel around. I imagine they have trouble with that slick clay when it rains. And the gravel was loose, so I had to be careful going down that steep slope.

But the gate was in good condition and did not sag. It was fastened by a big heavy chain—about two and a half feet of it. There was a padlock on the end of it to lock the gate at night or maybe when Bettye VanDyne went away. But just then the chain was holding the gate closed the way my grandfather's gate was always closed. That is, the chain was looped through the gate and the links were caught on a big nail on the gatepost. That way the animals can't get out, but anybody with business to do can get in and out without any trouble.

I unfastened the gate, went through, and then hooked it up behind me carefully.

The barn was down a little ways and over to the left, and that slope was a little difficult for an old lady that's not too steady on her feet even when the ground is level.

I was making it along the best I could, no doubt resembling a bag of sawdust, when I looked up and saw this young woman coming up from the house toward me. She had her head down and hadn't seen me yet. She had on a dirty old pair of blue jeans, sneakers, and a black blouse with the sleeves rolled up.

"Hello," I said kind of loud.

She looked up and saw me and immediately commenced to roll her sleeves down.

"Oh, don't roll down your sleeves. It's too hot." I said. She was standing there about twenty feet from me, and she just kept on rolling down her sleeves. So I knew why that poor thing was rolling those sleeves down.

Lizze Wheeler had said that Miss VanDyne was forty years old or more, but from the looks of her I would have guessed nearly sixty. Bad complexion—greasy hair that looked like it had not been combed all week. To express it in line with the business she was in, she just hadn't been curried yet. But it was her eyes that were really pitiful, great hollow things!

"I'm Harriet Gardner," I said. And it wasn't exactly a lie because that was my maiden name. But at this late date it is as good an alias as any. "They tell me you sell horses."

"Yes," she said, but she didn't look like she was eager to do so.

"Well, I promised my granddaughter that when she graduated from high school, I would buy her a horse; and now she is reminding me of it."

"You know anything about horses?" Miss VanDyne said.

"Indeed I do. I used to ride in the shows when I was a girl." And that was the truth.

"What kind of horse did you have in mind?"

"A bridle horse. With just a little spirit but not too much. My granddaughter hasn't been riding long. She thinks she can ride anything, but I wouldn't want to give her something that would throw her off."

Miss VanDyne was looking me over from head to foot and back again.

"That sorrel mare with the colt," I said, "she's a pretty thing. Is she a walker?"

That must have been the right thing to say because Miss VanDyne smiled and said, "That's my best mare, and isn't the foal a beauty?"

Well, with that as a hint, I talked on about the sorrel mare, and I know a little something about horses that I was able to work into the conversation. And after a while she called her stable boy and had him bring several of the horses on a halter so I could see them close to the fence. I looked at their legs and looked at their mouths and mostly looked wise and made a pretty good facsimile of somebody who knows about horses.

All the time, I was more interested in Bettye VanDyne than
was in the horses. She was so nervous, and her eyes were
unny.

I just talked along—trying to gain her confidence, you
now.

Finally she asked me if I would care for a drink.

I said yes, and so we went down to the house, where I sat
n the porch and she went in to mix the drinks. I had told her
ourbon on the rocks would be fine.

I was glad for an interval to look around.

The chair I was sitting in was all right—a little rickety, but
ll right. The other chair was a little rattan porch chair with
ome of the rattan loose, but that happens in the best of
umilies. The cushion, however, was ragged with some torn-
p foam rubber coming out.

The porch floor needed painting, and one of the posts
nowed signs of rot.

There were no flower beds—nothing to make the place
ook pretty. Either Bettye VanDyne had none of the family's
ncome, or she just didn't care. I thought of her meager body
nd haggard face. It was enough to make me cry.

I don't have a grandchild. That was all a lie. Lamar and I
ust had one son, and he was killed over Germany. That was
ne greatest sorrow I'll ever know. So with Lamar gone, I am
ll alone. But if I had had a granddaughter, she would not
ave been graduating from high school. She would have been
ne age of Bettye VanDyne. And while thirty-five or forty is
ot young, still there ought to be many, many more years
efore a woman is old.

Well, I was sitting there waiting for my drink and hap-
ened to look over to the side down beyond a kind of shed;
nd there was a man coming around the corner of that shed.

My heart just stopped.

I would have known that fellow anywhere. Of all the

people I had been watching through that telescope on Marga
ret's back porch, this was the one I could really identify—th
one I said reminded me of a Confederate veteran. Well, h
had the awfulest old mustache. And what was worse, he wa
the same one who was in Duncan Yardley's office the nigh
I went to that Gold Coast club down on Division Street. O
all the people connected with the Drover crowd, the onl
two who could recognize me were Duncan Yardley and thi
man.

Well, of course, after the show I made of myself that nigh
at the club, I didn't see how this fellow could help remember
ing me. And sure enough he did remember, as I soon foun
out.

Lord have mercy, what was I to do? My mother used t
say, "Always be a lady"; and it's usually a pretty good policy

So I said, "Good afternoon! Do you work here?"

And that was a silly thing to say. Why else would he b
there in work clothes and dirty old scuffed shoes?

He sort of grumbled something.

"I guess you love horses," I said.

He pushed right on by me into the house banging th
screen door behind him.

I was sure he had recognized me; so what on earth was
going to do? Keep your nerves steady, old girl, I told mysel
If he smelled a rat when he saw *me*, what would he think
I ran away just because I saw *him*?

Then Miss VanDyne came out of the house and handed m
a glass with a paper towel wrapped around it.

"I didn't have any more paper napkins," she said by wa
of excuse.

"Why, this is just fine!" I exclaimed. "It's so kind of yo
to think of doing this. Do you carry on this business alone?"

"Yes."

"And how did you happen to get into it?"

"Horses are the only things I really know."

"I imagine your family must have been horse-lovers from ay back."

"I have no family. After my mother died in seventy-five, e farm was mine. So I began breeding horses then. Business s not been too good, but it'll be better. I'm going to build e place up, put in a ring, do training—that kind of thing."

She talked of the future, but in a voice that was so dreary—ere was no dream.

"Do you not have any family at all?" I knew she had mily, and I wanted her to talk about it.

"Only cousins."

"Do they live near?" I waited for an answer, but none ume. I saw that I could not go further with that subject. I pped my whiskey slowly.

"My granddaughter will be here in August," I said. "I want er to ride the horse before I buy it, you understand."

My hostess said that was fine. I was at a loss to get more out f her. I asked her about her television reception, hoping that at would lead to something.

It turned out that she watched the serials, and we talked out that a little while. The one she liked especially was one at I do not watch. Apparently it has to do with glamorous eople living in Florida.

"I lived in Florida," she said. "It was wonderful down ere, but I had to leave. Daddy had boats. He had three of em and took people tarpon fishing. Mother sold the busi-ess, and we stayed on down there after Daddy died. But hen she died too, this was all that was left."

Once more the conversation petered out. And as my drink as finished, I got up to leave.

She walked with me up the lane.

I felt so sorry for her, and I think she knew it. Of course, ll along we had had this idea that whatever they were up to,

all those Drovers were probably in it together. And now wit
the "Confederate veteran" being there on Miss VanDyne
horse farm, it was a sure thing.

At that thought I looked around; there was the "Confeder
ate veteran" following us. I had the impression that he ha
made a sudden movement and thought maybe from the wa
he was holding his right hand behind his back that he migh
have a pistol. I said to myself, that's just imagination, don
pay any attention to it; but I was almost out of my mind.

All the same, I looked him in the eye and said, "It was nic
meeting you. Take good care of that horse I'm going to bu
for my granddaughter."

I was about to go up that slope to the gate, when th
thought came to me: What if this is the place where Mr
García was killed and they are going to kill me here too! Yo
see, that was the state I was in.

Well, I had to watch where I put my feet on that loos
gravel going up to the road. And Miss VanDyne had gon
ahead to open the gate. I looked up and saw her above me
the heavy chain in her hand. It was that image and fea
coming together in that way that suddenly galvanized m
imagination. I turned my eyes once more to the ground to ri
my mind of the thought that flashed there. I took a step—an
another step. I was not through the gate, but my eyes wer
still on the ground. Then the way the sun was shining, I sav
a little gleam.

My hand went to my throat. Pebbles rolled under my foo
and I sprawled on the ground as a strong jerk at my necklac
broke the cord and scattered the crystal beads everywhere.

"Oh, my! Oh, my!" I gasped.

Immediately I looked up and saw Bettye leaning over me
She seemed to be quite frightened. "Are you hurt?" sh
gasped.

I got myself into a sitting position and looked as dazed as
could.

I heard her say to that man I told you about, "Go back.
an't you see the poor thing is hurt?" And he did.

I said, "Oh, dear!" several times, partly because I *had* hurt
yself. I had scraped my shin almost raw. "No, I'm all right,"
said after a quick inspection. "But my beads!" I exclaimed.
They are cut crystal, and my husband gave them to me on
e day we were married."

I scrambled to my poor old knees and began to pick up the
eaming bits of glass and put them into my handbag.

"Darling, help me find them," I said as though I was
eartbroken over the loss of even one bead.

Well, we picked around in that gravel; and I picked more
arefully than you'd ever expect. It took more time than I
ked, I can assure you. But I had to make it look like I was
nly picking up little crystal beads.

Finally I decided that I had found all I was going to find.
thanked Bettye for her help and told her I would see her in
ugust. I got into my car and started up quick. I didn't even
rn around so as to go back the way I had come. No indeed.
just wanted to get shut of that place right away.

So I went fast as I could, although that road was just a snake
e way it wiggled around.

About the time I commenced to relax, I looked in the
arview mirror and saw this old gray automobile behind me,
oming fast. The thought struck me like a ton of bricks: What
it's him?

And it was.

Something said to me: Drive in the middle of the road so
e can't come up beside you.

And that's what I did.

He just stayed right there almost on my back bumper. I
ould step on the gas a little, and he would step on the gas

a little. I would slow down a little, and he would slow dow
a little. My old De Soto is thirty-five years old, but it hasn
gone over fifty thousand miles, and I figured it could
pretty fast and I could get away if that dratted road just hadn
been such a mass of curlicues.

Pretty soon I was relieved to see that the fellow was falli
back. I was just delighted.

Then I heard a gun.

And I realized that the reason he was falling back was so
could shoot at me when I went around a bend in the roa
I suppose he had to shoot with his left hand, and that was
blessing.

But what *was* I to do?

Then I saw this big old lumbering shape ahead of me.
was the garbage truck.

It was just blocking the road and going so slow. Well that
it, I thought. That fellow will get me for sure.

I guess I didn't tell you that all this time the road had bee
running through cutover timber where the new-growth pin
was about fifteen feet or so high, and it was just thick ever
where on both sides. That meant you couldn't see around
bend very far at all.

Well, I got around one of those curves, and what do yo
think? That garbage truck was turning off. We had come
the dump.

You can bet I followed that garbage truck right into th
dump. And there were three other trucks there and a ma
with one of those bulldozer things. I sailed right into th
midst of them and just sat tight.

The fellow in that gray car didn't know what to do. I sa
him drive by that entrance. And in a few minutes he drov
back the other way. Then he went by again. But he didn
dare come in because there were all those garbagemen there

can tell you they were the handsomest garbagemen I ever
xpect to see. I just loved them.

As you might expect, the trucks were there to dump garage and not to sit around. So one of them pulled out and
hen another. That left one truck and the bulldozer man. I
upposed some more trucks might come along, but there was
o assurance of that.

It was getting on past three o'clock, and I knew they would
ll be gone—including the bulldozer man—at five or maybe
ven four. And there I would be, back in a pickle again.

So I drove my car up next to the one garbage truck that was
till there and said to the driver, nice young man—looked like
e might be twenty-five or thirty—I said, "Can you tell me
f there is another way to get out of this dump except the way
came in?"

He had that machinery going that dumps the garbage and
idn't hear. So I asked him again.

"Yes ma'am," he said. "Hit's right through thataway." He
vas just a good old Tennessee boy. And he was pointing—it
ooked like—to a big pile of garbage that the man with the
ulldozer thing hadn't flattened out yet.

I pulled around in that direction, and sure enough, there
vas a way out over there.

Believe me, I took it and did not spare the horses!

After about ten minutes I was at Hogan's Tank. And I
new how to get back to Borderville from there. I guess my
Confederate veteran was still back there watching the en-
rance of that dump like a cat waiting for the mouse to come
ut of her hole—no, "his" hole. This women's lib thing has
ot me so mixed up I don't know what to say anymore. But
think the cat is female and the mouse is male, although it was
he other way around with me and that Confederate fellow.

I have a very fine man who takes care of my eyes—Dr.
Thomason. I absolutely think the world of him. He can do

just about anything that can be done in the line of eyeglasses
He has an office on Division Street, and there was a parking
place only three doors down from where he is.

Earlene Hawkes, the office girl, looked up when I came in
and of course knew me immediately—she should—I've been
going to Dr. Thomason for thirty years. "Why, I don't believe we have an appointment for you today, Mrs. Bushrow,"
she said.

"No, honey, you sure don't," I said. "This is something
different and something special. I've got a little job for Dr
Thomason to do for me and it won't take two minutes for me
to explain it to him."

He had a patient having his eyes examined, which means
I had to wait a little bit. And that was just as well because
had to dig around in my purse to find the evidence I had been
collecting. By the time Dr. Thomason's patient was out of the
office, I had got together four pretty good pieces of lens and
two tiny slivers.

"Can you tell me what the formula for a lens is by looking
at broken pieces?" I asked after Dr. Thomason had greeted
me.

"Perhaps," he said. "It depends on the condition and size
of the pieces."

"All right, then," I said. "Here are the pieces."

"But Mrs. Bushrow," he objected, "we have your prescription on file. We would not have to reconstruct it from
these pieces."

I looked at him and laughed. "Who said these are from my
prescription?"

He looked at me in a quizzical sort of way.

"Now, don't ask questions," I said. "Ladies have their
secrets." And I gave him such a look that it would have
melted his heart if I had been sixty years younger. It doesn'
have the same effect when you are eighty-six, but at least Dr

Thomason took the little pieces of glass and said he would let me know by Thursday.

Between my adventure and the whiskey Bettye VanDyne had given me, I was revved up. I hardly noticed the pain in my shin as I drove home, and it really wasn't all that bad. I put a little salve on it, and went straight to the telephone to call Helen Delaporte.

"I want you to find out something for me from those folks out in California," I said. And then I told her what I wanted. And of course I had to tell all about my adventure. Helen was horrified, but that was all right.

I don't know when I have been so excited about anything. But, then, if I was all wrong, what a fool I would look!

I made myself a little supper and tried to watch TV. I got ready for bed and turned out the light. In the darkness I could imagine Bettye VanDyne holding a length of chain about two feet long with a heavy padlock hanging from the end. It was an eerie picture like the posters that used to advertise horror movies. Poor little Bettye! The stuff that had made a monster of her would make a monster of anybody.

HOW THE TENNESSEE SHERIFF'S DEPARTMENT TOOK OVER THE CASE

Helen Delaporte

From the moment Henry laid down the law, I fully intended to have nothing more to do with gumshoe work of any kind. And in fact I never touched the matter except to use the telephone. To that extent I disobeyed Henry's injunction, but I suppose it is forgivable casuistry to claim that using the telephone is not the same thing as talking to someone face to face.

Whatever the conjugal blame I deserve, as soon as the rates went down, I called Hornsby Roadheaver and got from him the telephone number of the little harpist who had been the assistant of García in his school. He knew her number without consulting a telephone book or memorandum of any kind. So apparently one good thing was resulting from this murder.

Miss Sieburg was at home, and wonder of wonders, she knew the name of the opthalmologist. After a glance at her directory, she had the address and telephone number for me. So that was very easily done.

But Miss Sieburg had never known Evelyn García. That meant that I had to call Ethel Muehlbach. Although Ethel did not have the answer, she said she would ask around.

When I told Henry about all of this, he was incredulous but charmed that a woman of Harriet's age should have become so involved in an affair of this sort. He doubted that the bits of glass would turn out to match García's prescription. But then he had not heard Harriet explain how she had collected those bits of glass from the gravel right under the nose of her prime suspect.

"But if it should be García's prescription?" I asked. I so wanted Harriet to have solved the case!

"A lens is not the same thing as a fingerprint," Henry said. "You would need supporting evidence." And we left it at that.

I called Harriet, gave her the address of the oculist she wanted, and told her that Ethel would find out what she could and call me.

Then Henry and I went away to the beach for four days. On the day after we got back, I got a call from Harriet.

"Where have you been?" (This in a rather accusing tone.)

"Hilton Head."

"I know it was lovely. Are you sunburned?"

"A little."

"You haven't heard from the lady friend in California, have you?"

"No, I haven't. And there was nothing from California on our answering machine."

There was a pause. "Oh, I was hoping you might have heard."

There was such disappointment in that sentence that I felt a wretch not to have received a call. I promised Harriet that I would call Ethel that very night.

So I talked to Ethel. It was one of those things where

nobody was quite sure. General talk had it that Evelyn García had died of a heart attack, but one of the women who had played bridge with her said it was drugs.

The trouble had started when García had gone on extended tours and Evelyn had been alone. She was very dependent and lost without him. When García returned, Evelyn had tried to keep the habit from him and seemed to have succeeded, but her bridge friends suspected; and if the husband knew about it, he was too proud to let the addiction of his wife become common gossip. So they watched it and saw that some times were better and some times worse. Her health declined and her appearance was such that when she died, it was quite believable by the public at large that she had died of heart disease. But Ethel's informant was quite sure that it was either an overdose or cardiac arrest in some manner related to the habit.

"I knew it," Harriet declared jubilantly when I told her. "I don't know how, but I knew it.

"Just wait," she continued, "We'll have real news in a few days."

We needed the answer from the oculist. I was confident that Harriet had ferreted out the solution, but it all hinged on those two things.

In a little less than a week the prescription arrived from Santa Barbara. After Harriet conferred with Dr. Thomason, she called me again. "Helen, do you think your husband could listen to me a little while if I came by your house at a convenient time?"

I assured her he could and would. And in fact I suggested that she join us for dinner at Ted's.

"Ted's!" she said. "How nice!"

So we met her at 7:30 in Ted's parking lot.

"Now, there will be no talking about anything consequential," Henry announced, "until after we have finished dinner."

And so we only talked of *in*consequential things until the dessert had been served. Meanwhile, I am bound to observe that Harriet flirted shamelessly with Henry. And Henry loved it.

After the coffee had been replenished, Henry turned to Harriet and said. "Now let us talk about things consequential."

"Very well," said Harriet as dispassionately as though she had been asked to open the bidding.

"As you know, Mr. Delaporte, your wife led us into a very puzzling and intriguing adventure.

"From the very beginning she recognized that there had been an attempt to hide both the identity of the deceased and the place of his murder. Through her cleverness, Helen established Mr. García's identity. But it didn't make any sense at all for a great, famous musician to come to a place like Borderville and nobody would know about it. And then for a perfect stranger—and it certainly looked as if Mr. García was a perfect stranger, at least to anybody around here—for a perfect stranger to be murdered! The question is why anybody around here would have something against him that would call for killing the poor man. And it was perfectly ridiculous that he should be killed out there in that Brown Spring Cemetery.

"Then by accident our Helen learned that there was a connection between Mr. García and the Drover family, and she saw that we would have to investigate the whole family from old Quinby Drover down to the present.

"That's when little Lizzie Wheeler got to work and made that chart of the Drovers with all their laws and in-laws. But looking at the Drover family tree didn't seem to suggest any reason to murder Mr. García."

Harriet paused to take a sip from her coffee cup. "Well, some of us," she resumed, "knew a thing or two about old Quinby and the rest of the Drover crew. And those of us with the longest memories wouldn't be surprised at anything, because that old man was a scoundrel.

"Lizzie did a marvelous job of tracing the family—with dates and everything—and it turned out that there were only five living Drovers, so to speak, and Mr. García would have made the sixth. There was Allen Comming, Jr., Duncan Yardley, and Dorothy Greene Raebon, Dr. Anthony Hancock, and Bettye VanDyne.

"It was like looking at a pack of cards and knowing that somewhere there was the ace of spades.

"Well, there was the map that Lizzie had found and the dark pencil line showing that whoever had taken García's body out to Brown Spring had not known where the cemetery was. And then there was the other thing: We also turned up the fact that there were Baker graves out there and the Bakers are Allen's mother's people.

"That made it look as though Allen Comming had had something to do with the disposal of the body, and so he was a party to the murder or perhaps just involved in some distant way.

"Then Helen carried the investigation of the family a step further. She went to Angus Redloch, who knew all about the will but also pretty much how the family fortune was dissipated. And I could bear witness to much of that myself, because I was right here when most of it went up the spout.

"We all know that Allen came home from the Vietnam War and took over the management of Borderville Transfer, which was just about all the wealth that had come through the depression for the Drover heirs, and there is no doubt that he improved the business. But then there was a time in the late fifties when his father built that storage warehouse up on the hill, and he would have had to borrow money for that. So Allen, Jr., may have had to pay that off; I imagine he did.

"Now who of us knows whether that transfer business is

making money? After watching that enterprise for the better part of a month, frankly I saw little that would make me believe that Allen Comming can support his life-style from Borderville Transfer. But both Allen Comming and Duncan Yardley seem to have plenty of money.

"That's how things stood when Opal Ledbetter made her national defense report for the May meeting of the chapter. And that triggered a memory. It came to me that Duncan Yardley must be the operator of the Gold Coast."

Harriet began to fumble in her famous pocketbook. "Do you mind if I smoke?" she said.

I don't know why the question should have surprised me. Neither Henry nor I smoke, and I had known Harriet for such a long time without ever having seen her with a cigarette that I felt just a bit shocked at her request. I could tell that Henry too was taken by surprise as he reached for the matchbook in its holder between the salt and pepper shakers.

Harriet looked up with a mischievous grin. "Well, I'm not going to smoke," she said as she extracted something wrapped in Kleenex from her purse. She handed it to him. "That's the evidence," she said. "That's where the Drover money comes from today. From these marijuana cigarettes and the other stuff he has in those little plastic packets I saw in his safe while I was in his office down at the Gold Coast. And I believe we will find that he is in the dope business much deeper than that.

"Meanwhile," Harriet continued, "at Helen's suggestion, Margaret Chalmers and I took up our post watching the Borderville Transfer premises. We found a very strange pattern. Every so often, about seven or seven-thirty in the evening, a car from the south—always from the south—would roll up that hill and drive right into the warehouse. Then the next day, early, three cars would sort of converge, go into the warehouse for a while, and then come out and go off different ways. Then in five or six days the same thing would happen again.

"Now you can't tell me they weren't distributing something.

"Then Helen saw this Highsmith fellow wearing a suede jacket that she thought belonged to García. And when the police began looking for that jacket, what should happen but somebody shot Highsmith out there on four-twenty-one.

"And they almost shot our little Helen." Harriet leaned over and patted me on the arm.

"At that point we had pretty good evidence that both Duncan Yardley and Allen Comming were in the dope business, but I didn't see how we were going to prove that either of them had killed Luís García.

"Well, I thought, we haven't investigated Bettye VanDyne the way we have snooped around those boys, and she's right here in the county. So I went out there.

"It's a very pitiful thing; that place is so poorly kept up. That girl isn't making anything there. And I hadn't been talking to her ten minutes before I knew she was on drugs.

"It was just very sad. And yet—you can't just let a murderer go.

"Then that man—I call him the 'Confederate veteran'— came around the corner, and he must have known in a minute who I was. So I was eager to get away from there and mostly from him.

"While Miss VanDyne was opening the gate to let me out, two things happened almost at the same time. I saw the broken lens of García's glasses, for one thing."

Harriet delved into her purse once more and came up with a rumpled envelope. "Here are the pieces. Dr. Thomason worked out the prescription from the fragments. It turned out that there are parts of two lenses here. One was a prescription lens, and the other was not a lens at all, which, if you'll think about it, is the way it would have to be, since the poor man was blind in one eye. Helen got me the address of Mr. García's ophthalmologist in California so I could write out there and check it. According to the prescription he sent me, these are Mr. García's lenses. And I would think that that means that Mr. García was killed right there at Bettye Van-Dyne's gate.

"Now, for the other thing that came to me just at the time I saw the glint of the glass among the pebbles—Bettye Van-Dyne was standing there holding the chain that ordinarily keeps the gate shut. It was then that I first thought of her as a menacing figure. That poor girl is very strange. If she was hopped up on something, she could swing that chain with that great big padlock on the end of it, and she could kill somebody with it. And I don't suppose that it would take too much to crush a man's windpipe with a heavy chain swinging around like that.

"And, of course, if you think about it, most folks would protect their face and eyes with their hands. But, no, with Mr. García, all that was different. Those artist's hands of his meant more to him than his eyes. So he didn't raise his hands, and so that chain with that big lock on it just hit him and hit him. I don't know whether she actually hit his glasses or they fell off and got stepped on and broken. I suppose somebody picked up what was left of the frames—they would be easy to see. And maybe they took the pieces of glass that were easiest to find."

Harriet paused. "I've been talking too much," she said. "Let me get a sip of water."

Henry gave me that look he gives when he is impressed, and I was as proud of Harriet as I could be. After this, Henry would have to take my "old ladies" much more seriously than he had before.

"Now, there's one other thing," Harriet began again. "I believe that they always require a motive in detective stories and in murders and things like that. Well, Helen sniffed out that one too. Evelyn Haverty García was an addict and died as a result of her addiction. Helen learned that from her friend in Santa Barbara, California.

"The way I see this, Mr. García was a man of fine gentlemanly instincts. A man like that, and with a sense of honor and all that, such as they say the Spanish have, would never accept the death of a loved one by drugs. Why, that's borne out by the way he let it seem that she had died of heart trouble.

"Just consider the position he was in. I don't know how the Drovers divvy up the proceeds from their drug business, but according to Angus Redloch, Evelyn Haverty would have been getting some income from the family business, namely the Borderville Transfer. But we know that for all intents and purposes there is not much legitimate transfer business going on at that place. And when Evelyn died and García inherited, why, that made Luís García a participant in whatever was going on over there at Borderville Transfer.

"Now, suppose that in some way—and I don't know that we will ever find out how—Mr. García got wind of the drug operation. Maybe it had something to do with the variation in how the money was coming to him, or maybe he was just wondering why he was not getting any money—however it might be, if he ever got such a notion, how would he react? How would you react to that, Mr. Delaporte?"

It was a rhetorical question, and Henry did not have to answer; for Harriet went on immediately: "I think he did just what you would have done—Mr. García came to Borderville to investigate. It wouldn't be too hard to find out that something fishy was going on.

"There is no way we can know how he got his information, but let's just say that he went out to Bettye VanDyne's place to see if she would cooperate with him, and let's say that he found that she was on dope.

"All right! I imagine he pointed out to her what she was doing to herself. And then he probably went on to point out what the drug trade was doing to thousands of young people everywhere. And then I think maybe some kind of quarrel broke out and she realized he would go to the authorities, and that was when she struck him with the chain.

"Now have I got that right?" Harriet demanded.

Henry rubbed his chin. "You have made a case," he said. "Where is this farm of Miss VanDyne's?"

"Down here about ten miles out of town."

"On which side?"

"Tennessee."

"That's good," Henry said. "We don't have to deal with Gilroy and Jefferson; they are on the Virginia side. If you want me to, I'll take your evidence and lay it before the Tennessee authorities. There is certainly enough here to call for an investigation."

"Now, hold on a minute," Harriet said. "I don't want you going in there after poor Bettye in such a way that while the police are investigating her, the other Drovers can get away and leave the country. After all, Miss VanDyne probably saved my life; and she killed only one man, but just look at the lives that have been ruined by the narcotics trade."

"The federal officers will take care of the narcotics angle," Henry said.

"Oh, that's good." Harriet was all smiles—almost as if she had won a bridge tournament.

All told, it was undoubtedly the most extraordinary dinner conversation Henry and I will ever experience. He went right home and made an appointment to see Glenn Martin, the Tennessee sheriff, the next morning at 9:00.

It was a week before the arrests took place. The federals made a raid on the warehouse and the Gold Coast simultaneously. Both places proved to be very interesting.

Allen Comming was in his office down at the foot of the hill below the warehouse at Borderville Transfer. At the warehouse itself, the officers found a man in the act of taking three hundred packets of cocaine from the upholstery of the backseat of a car with a Florida license plate. And they caught three couriers, one of them apparently a new man who had taken the place of Highsmith.

Yardley was arrested at his home, and the raid on the Gold Coast yielded drugs of various description—quite enough to keep him in the penitentiary for many years.

Meanwhile, the sheriff's men were watching Bettye Van-Dyne's farm. Only a few minutes after Allen Comming's arrest, Betty ran out of the house and got into an old gray Plymouth. The deputies were waiting for her at the gate.

They brought her to the jail and questioned her for three hours before they got her complete confession.

The newspapers went wild. They had the story from the Tennessee sheriff's office, and they wanted a statement from me because the affair had been so often referred to as the DAR Murder Mystery. Elizabeth Wheeler's friend Mr. Manley called me right away. "No," I said, "I don't wish to make a statement. But I am sure you can get a very good story from Mrs. L. Q. C. Lamar Bushrow."

Bettye VanDyne was let out on bail, and the following day her stable boy found her body. She had deliberately taken an overdose, and she had left a suicide note, a copy of which I shall now insert into this record.

"If anybody cares," it began,

> "Daddy first got into the drug traffic in 1955. He was in debt very deeply and tried to raise money through Uncle Baker Comming. Tony Hancock found out about it. He had been prescribing narcotics illegally for years and knew about a man called Herbert Donaldson in

Florida. Donaldson set Daddy up with three boats and a fishing venture as a cover for drug running. It was not a big operation then, and Daddy was only involved in bringing the stuff—hash, pot, coke, whatever—to shore at different places.

"One time Daddy couldn't make his rendez-vous ashore where it had been planned because of a storm, and he put into Lauderdale, where we lived then.

"I was in high school, and that night I was driving around with a bunch of kids through the storm and said, "Let's go down to the boats."

"Daddy was sleeping off a drunk, so we scrambled all over that boat and found the drugs. That was the first time I ever shot up.

"It went on from there. When Daddy died in '68, I realized I would have to do something about the habit. So I checked into a clinic down there. It was really bad, but I got through it all right and knocked the habit for a while.

"Then I got on it again and had a really bad experience. I went to the same clinic and took the cure. But I just went back to drugs again. I took the cure a third time, and it was the same old story.

"I know now that I am hooked forever. I don't have the strength to go through a clinic again, and I know it wouldn't do any good if I did.

"When Mother died, I inherited her part of the Drover estate. That brought me in close contact with Allen Comming. He had been running the business for several years, and it just fell apart in 1973. He was in big debt and didn't know what to do, when Tony Hancock told him how to get contact with Donaldson. With Allen it was a choice between joining the operation and taking bankruptcy. Allen, Jr., took over when his father died in 1975, and Duncan Yardley came in on the deal later.

"Those two bastards took all the money for themselves. I was lucky if I got fifteen hundred a year. They said it came from the transfer business. Then to keep me quiet they let me have all the coke, pot, anything I wanted.

"I could have done really well if I had been willing to be a dealer. But I knew what drugs do to people, and I just couldn't bring myself to sell misery to those poor saps out there. So Allen and Dunk gave me any of the merchandise I wanted just to keep me quiet.

"I always loved horses. The only real pleasure I have had these last years has been seeing my colts grow into big, beautiful animals.

"Last February when Lu García came out to the farm, he had some idea that he could get me to help him force Allen out of the racket. He was standing at the gate and said that he could stop it all with the law.

"I panicked. I just could not go through withdrawal again. The chain with the lock on it was on the ground just at my feet. I picked it up and in a rage struck out at Lu. He was above me, and I had to reach to strike at his face. The first time I hit him, his foot slipped on the gravel and he fell. I hit him again and again.

"When he didn't move, I knew he was dead.

"It was a dark night, and the body had rolled

down the hill, where car lights would not touch it even if someone drove by.

"I stood there a long time. Then I went into the house, and it was about half an hour before I could think what to do. I called Allen. And he called Tony Hancock.

"Tony always comes to Borderville when Allen and Duncan want to talk business. He's afraid of wiretaps.

"In about twenty minutes Allen came and put the body in his station wagon. He took it to the warehouse to wait for Tony.

"When Tony got there, he told Allen to have Joe Highsmith dump the body in the lake. So Allen got Joe up and had him take the body in the station wagon out to the bridge. But there was too much traffic on 421 to throw it from the bridge, and the lake was so low at that time that he couldn't drive down to the water without getting stuck in the clay. So he brought the body back.

"Meanwhile Allen brought Duncan into it. He was the one who thought of planting the body in that cemetery. They told Joe to burn Lu's clothes; and he did, all except the jacket.

"It has been a lousy life. I am writing this so that someone will know not just what I did, but why I did it. When I started out, I certainly didn't mean for it to end this way. I was suckered into it. It was the same with Allen and Dunk. Drugs just got to be the family business.

"The one who caused it all was Tony Hancock, and I only hope that if I go to hell (and I guess I will), I'll see him there, because I have a score to settle with him."

The federals had already learned from Bettye's confession at the jail that Hancock was very much a part of the drug ring. And they had notified the officers in Roanoke to pick him up. But he had already heard the news, and he and his nurse had disappeared.

All of this was swirling around us when all sorts of reporters and photographers hit town. There was a team from Knoxville, and even one from Atlanta. They came out to our house.

"Don't interview me," I said. "Interview Harriet Bushrow, Margaret Chalmers, and Elizabeth Wheeler." And that is what they did.

The Knoxville photographer got a picture of the three standing on Margaret's front porch. But the photographer from Atlanta was really clever. He photographed the three ladies in the pose of Grant Wood's painting known as *Daughters of the American Revolution;* and that is the picture that was copied all over the country.

EXCERPT FROM THE MINUTES OF THE SEPTEMBER
MEETING OF THE OLD ORCHARD
FORT CHAPTER, NSDAR

Mrs. Bushrow reported that as a direct result of the investigation carried out by herself and Mrs. Ledbetter, the exhibition of male striptease dancing has ceased and the Gold Coast nightclub has been closed.